Waterford
And Nearby Towns

Owen Knight

Illustrated by
Martine Khadr-Van Schoote

LEFTHANDPRESS

A DIVISION OF BLACK MOON PUBLISHING, LLC
CINCINNATI, OHIO USA

Black Moon Manifesto

*It is the Will and mission of Bate Cabal/Black Moon to
effectively manifest unique and insightful occult Works
for the esoteric community in a manner that is unfettered
by commercial considerations.*

BlackMoonPublishing.com

blackmoonpublishing@gmail.com

Design and layout by
Jo Bounds of Black Moon

ISBN: 978-1-890399-83-2
United States • United Kingdom • Europe • Australia • India • Japan

With a huge thank you to

Micha Pollick,

Cliff Pollick, and Emily Baehr, for getting

Waterford and Nearby Towns copied for publication.

and to

Emily Baehr for getting

Wind Over Linden Hill

and *Waterford and Nearby Towns* into book form.

—Owen

CONTENTS

Illustrations:

Under the Simes

Aunt Maud stands in the door in the warm sunlight. A faint smile can be seen to cross her lips. Short, dark Aunt Maud stares in to space and chuckles silently to herself. The porch squeaks to the seemingly endless rocking of old ladies rocking. The squeak of the rocking is mixed with the soughing of the wind, with the babble of talk, the talking of the old ladies.

Farzie is walking up the lane, moving one stiff leg slowly and listening to Mister Avery who is shouting something into Farzie's ear.

The chickens cackle. The cows moo. The farm buzzes in the sunshine hot morning. Under the lindens, in a wooden chair; Muzzie, my grandmother, is sitting with my sister and singing; in an old voice, "The buzzards and the butterflies are picking out its eyes"... Up in the lindens, the locusts are singing, "Pharaoh, Pharaoh, let my people go."

The wind swirls over the hill. The lindens shake and sigh. I sit in the ham mock and watch the linden between me and the grey front porch lift a leafy arm to disclose, in the trunk, a dark mysterious hole going inward into a black pit. The leafy arm came down. The tree was back its normal self again. Over the low roof of the long grey weathered house blows the wind. Over the low, paintless house, the lindens bend and sway. The wind swings the triangle which hangs on the long front porch; the porch raised just a few inches above the ground. The wind blows away. All is still. The old boards squeak with the rocking chairs. Old ladies: Miss Lizzie, Sister, Sister Lucie, sit rocking. Somewhere, there is the coo coo of a mourning dove. Aunt Maud looks out over the hills, looks past the grey, sagging barns, past where sunny patterns on fields melt into blue haze; looks out to a distance where fields, hills and sky go on forever.

In the hammock I lie contemplating the shifting, speckled patterns of sunlight in the tufts of hairy, brownish green grass and the babble of talking coming from the front porch, the talking now mixed with the soughing of the wind. And the bobbing, leafy arm, raising to reveal a dark round hole. Then, down again. In a sigh of wind, the linden bends its top. On the other side of me a linden bends. And the scraggly locust trees down past the front gate.

A tall, thin man, Cousin Cornelius, comes out the library door, out onto the porch. He rings the triangle.

I get out of the hammock, run up to the porch, go in the dining room door, go past the long table set with china and bright silverware; go to my right, into the room with the blank faced, eyeless, terra cotta angels, above the door. From a large, pale china pitcher; I pour cool water into the china washbowl; wash; then, go into the dining room, go up to my place at the table. People take their places. Farzie raises his hand.

"Bless, O Lord, these thy gifts to us and us to thy service.."

Farzie carves the meat. Dishes rattle as bowls of vegetables are passed.

"... so they reminded those of us who had any interest...", Cousin Gracie is saying.

I am served to a helping of string beans. Aunt Binty puts them on my plate, passes the dish on. Now, lots of people are talking.

" ... And then I became aware, and you knot it now, that of course..." Aunt Binty is saying.

Uncle Faust and Cousin Cornelius are laughing over something.

"Now, Faust, I know you'll have more corn", Aunt Hannah is saying.

The sunlight shines through the wavy glass in the window, falls in bright spots on the white tablecloth, on the blue patterned and greybrown patterned serving dishes. It plays off the cut glass cruets, off the brown pepper mill and glistens off the silverware. It shines off Farzie's black silk cap. The splotchy, brownish orange plaster and grey, paintless woodwork of the door frames pick up the bright, midday light. Beside the fireplace, cupboards stand dark and tall and over the fireplace hangs the dark picture of fruit falling over the rim of a basket shaped like a horn. People are talking. Dishes are passed around. On the other side of the table sits Uncle Alba with his long stem face, sits Uncle Faust, his wide mough filled with teeth. The sun shines off his horn rimmed spectacles. Sister, a tall thin, wrinkled lady, is saying something to Muzzie. Up next to Farzie sits Sister Nancy with her topknot of white hair.

Sister Lucky is saying, " ... do say so? Well, I declare. Well I never."

Everyone eats. I eat as I listen to the quiet voices around the table.

The plates are cleared away and bread pudding in small, blue and white dishes is brought in. Sister says, " ... Well that's the funniest thing I ever... "

I eat my pudding. The family gets up. Some go out on the porch. I follow Muzzie, Miss Lizzie, Cousin Gracie and Aunt Binty into the room of the angels. Near the cold stove sits Aunt Binty. Beside her, the authoritative Cousin Gracie sedately sits. Muzzie sits on the others side of the stove, her long face tilted sideways to hear what Aunt Binty is saying. Next to Muzzie sits the dignified Miss Lizzie peering through nose glasses set close to her eyes and tilted to her left. She nods and smiles quizzically as the ladies talk.

Aunt Binty speaks, speaks quietly while she holds in her right hand a heavy, dark cane. Her hair is done up on top of her head in a grey topknot. To the right of Miss Lizzie, left of where Sister Lucy sits, is a small table and on it, an unlit, clear glass oil lamp. Against the right wall, to the left of the window, stood the pitcher and bowl on the marbletop wash stand. Muzzie's head is tilted sideways so that it catches, from the window, a halo of light. The light falls brightly on Muzzie's smile. Over the dining room door are the pair of blank faced, eyeless angels. They look down on the people in the room. They keep silent.

I walked under the eyeless angels, into the dining room; walked down , through the door into the dark kitchen with the smoky wooden beams. I went around the great iron wood range, climbed up the dark, narrow, curving stairs to Sister Nancy's room. The door is open. I go in. In a chair under the window sits Sister Nancy, sewing. I go to the stand near the door where on rows of curvy shelves are rows of pretty things. I stand and look at them.

"Would you like to play with the little animals?" Sister Nancy asks.

"Yes please."

I select a red pottery dog and a smaller animal; a black stone cat with diamond eyes, put them on a small, round cloth rug. The cloth goes round and round like braided paths. Sister Nancy, with a faint, thin smile, sits and sews. A mound of white hair sits on her head and around her eyes are dark rings. Sunlight comes in the window and falls on the rug. I put the animals in the patch of sunlight. Out the window I can see the bright sky. Along the wall left of the window, the bed is neatly made up with a bright spread. To the right of Sister Nancy, along the wall, in the shadow, is a spinning wheel which nobody uses. To the right, beyond the spinning wheel, is the door to the dark room. I watch the darkroom door, not getting too close, as the darkness might creep out under the door. No one goes into the darkroom.

I get up, put the animals back in their places.

"Thank you, Sister Nancy."

I go out into the hall, down the dark stairs to the kitchen, go into the vestibule, then through the door into the library where, against the walls, stand tall bookcases filled with rows of books. I pass where Farzie, in his huge chair, sits reading by the huge fireplace. I go out on the porch. The dust from the fields covers the porch and the porch chairs. It floats down in a column of sunlight. In the back fields, haystacks catch the sunlight. A rickety hay wagon moves slowly across the east field, shakes, shakes as it goes.

I wander into the yard, under the maple. Wallace, a stooped coloured man with a beat up hat and grey moustache, is on the other side of the fence.

"Wallace", I ask, "Why is your moustache so grey?" "It's cause. Ah war bomed afore dem."

"Before what?"

"Simes," Wallace whispers to me.

He walks on toward the back.

I go over to the hammock, sit and listen to the wind blowing in the trees. Great White clouds, billowy masses, sail over. More billowy clouds sail up. There is Uncle Faust coming up from the horse barn, looking darkly through horn rimmed spectacles. He walks up to Farzie.

"There's something wrong with the horses," he hollers in Farzie's ear. "They act dead."

Farzie looks thoughtful, says nothing,. He is standing by some large rocks where the ground slopes down sharply on the west side of the house.

Now I see Uncle Alba standing under the lower linden, talking to Uncle Teunis. Uncle Teunis stands with his thumbs in his pockets, his head bent down. He was watching the ground in front of his feet and a half scowl is on his long, greying face. He seems deep in thought.

I go up to them.

"Uncle Teunis, what are simes?"

"Hush," Uncle Alba sternly says in a half whisper and fixes hard, accusing eyes on me. Uncle Teunis says nothing, but his face gets longer than ever.

The lindens rock in the wind, raising and lowering their branches, their great limbs. Upstairs, up the twisting black, smoked stairs hidden behind the kitchen wall, sits Sister Nancy spinning, her grim face staring blankly into nothing while the wheel hums. She sits stiffly. Under a mass of white hair, her dark eyes are so dark and sunken that they seem like they aren't there, that nothing's in the large, dark brown circles. Her features are sharp and determined as she spins. As she spins and spins; shadow, like green mould, streaks half her pale face.

I stand on the porch and watch the linden giants, lopsided in the wind. I look up at the sky, at the stars. The sky is filled with moons, not stars; big, round things staring down.

Wallace sneaks up on the porch, cowers in the comer. "Wallace, look at all those moons."

Wallace, trembling, says, "Them ain't moons. Them's simes."
"Come in here." I heard Uncle Alba's harsh whisper.

Most of the family is in the room of the angels. Uncle Teunis is standing by the stove, his face getting longer and longer. Everyone looks worried, but Sister Nancy isn't there. She is up in her room. She looks grimly into space. I go past Uncle Teunis, out the door behind the stove, onto the old grey boards of the porch to the dairy. I walk up through the yard to see the patch of sweet petunias behind the chicken house, but bounce up and down as I walk on the ground which feels like coils of springs. Over head, the hundreds of simes smile down looking at th1.ngs. I'm on a path I've never seen before. Tall trees, on either side, lead to a tall frame house, a dull faded red house which rises through the trees. Tall as the trees, it has tall, dark slits for windows which watch me come up the road. Inside is cold, dark air and an organ inside, long planks over an awful organ. I try to go back, buy my legs go up and down on the springs. I go up and down under the simes which are looking down. Back on the grey boards of the porch to the dairy, I go back into the room of the angels. I'm on the steps to the cellar. The dirt cellar steps have springs inside. So does the cellar floor where the piano is and Uncle Alba is lying on the keys of the piano. His body is split open and Uncle Faust is pulling out layer after layer of sponges, sponges of many colours like the piano has inside of it. The piano thing is turning its sponges and Uncle Faust is taking more coloured sponge out of Uncle Alba, more coloured sponge.

In the sky, the simes are getting dim. The house creaks. There is a greyness in my room. I see, beyond the window, the pale sky. In the fading mist of night, I see the fading outline of Uncle Alba looking sterner and colder than ever and Miss Lizzie's quizzical smile and the tilted nose glasses on her perpetually bobbing head, perpetually bobbing.

At The Office

The Sizemore Report

I sat reading, my chair pushed back from my desk. Dr. Armstrong sat reading one of my papers.

"Baliles, what's a sallygaster?

"I put down everything, as far as I know, which I was told. It seems to have been a bird like monster, one of the many subjects of mountain folk tales."

"They sound interesting. You know, this could be a more extensive, more elaborate project."

Dr. Armstrong got up from his desk and stood by the window. "The origins and current use of the folk tales of our mountains". He walked around to the front of his desk, leaned against the near comer, took the pipe out of his mouth. "Perhaps a little trip into those hills — I know we can get lost in folklore, but we are emphasizing their current rendition — quite a different approach — yes, come in, Miss Martindale."

"There's a Mr. Everett Sizemore to see you," said the tall, pleasant looking young woman, standing in the doorway.

"Have him come in," said the slender, grey haired, balding gentleman who at the moment, stopped leaning on the comer of his desk.

A reddish faced gentleman, with wavy grey hair, came in.

"Mr. Sizemore, I'm Dr. Armstrong. This is my associate, Dr. Baliles." He waved his hand toward where I sat.

"Good afternoon gentlemen. Dr. Armstrong, I have some events I'd like to relate. They are somewhat newsworthy."

13

"Mr. Sizemore, our usual procedure is to allow other publications to print newsworthy events. Then we select and analyze the events published by other publica tions. We make no effort to publish a news magazine. And our publication isn't a current events report; nor, am I particularly interested·in current events, as such; but in only those which have a significant effect upon society; its habits, philosophies, tactics; events whose effects and ramifications go back and forth across a period of time,"

"The events I've come to tell have had, and I believe, will continue to have an effect on the religion of certain isolated areas."

"In that case, we might be interested. Won't you tell them, please to Baliles here. He's been doing a rundown on religious type things. I have the threads in my brain all tied up in crime and punishment; and besides, it's my suppertime." Dr. Armstrong walked over, plucked his derby off the tall coat rack, put it on over his square grey moustache.

"Good night, Mr. Sizemore. Good night, Albion." "Good night, Mack," I said.

Dr. Armstrong went out.

"I'm interested in events," I said.

"I'm glad of that. I have them all written down here. I like your office I see you all, like I do, like to puts lots of odds and ends on your desks."

"Mostly on mine. Yes, I like my playthings. lpick up odds and ends as I travel about." "That's an interesting statue."

"I'm fond of it. It is a Chinese demigod carved in, I think, the Ming Dynasty." "Know anything about the god?"

"Not much. I just call him Ming. His spirit has been forced into the body of an old beggar and he is forced to live as such, an eternal beggar."

"Sounds like fun. You get it in China?"

"In Hong Kong. I got the book ends there in Manila. The Egyptian god I got in Port Said."

"The pagoda there come from Hong Kong too?"

"No, I just bought that the other day in a Chinese store here in

14

town. Would you drag up a chair and let me look over some of your papers; or, let me hear about them? Or would they go better over a beer; say, at the Old Ebbitt?"

"You know, I believe they would. I believe my story would tell better over a beer; or, over the porter that they serve down at the Old Ebbitt. Let's take them to the Ebbitt. Call me Everett."

"Splendid. Then let's go on down. I'm Albion."

I got up. We walked out of the office past Jennifer Martindale's desk.

Jennifer's desk chair was now occupied by a thin faced man in large, horn rimmed spectacles.

"Come on Quirk, we're going to the Old Ebbitt. Everett here is going to tell us about some interesting events. Everett, this is Anthony Quirk: Quirk, Everett Sizemore. Quirk doesn't like Anthony and he doesn't like Tony, so we just call him Quirk. You don't mind him listening in do you? Quirk is one of our publication's few part time employees."

"No, not at all. Nice to see you, sir." The two men shook hands.

The three of us walked out the outer office door, down the hall.

Faith, Agnosticism, Atheism
and Mermaids of the Nanticoke

As I piece the tale together from the account which Mr. Sizemore has given; for a start, we have an old Dodge sedan chugging down a remote country road. Four doctors of physics occupy the back seat; Dr. Owen Kavanagh on the left; a large fleshy Bostonian with blue eyes and wavy, dark hair; on the right, a tall, balding Baltimorean, Dan Fleckenstein. Between them; left, New Yorker Estel Flytell and right, Carolinian Henry Fogwell. Up front, Mr. Sizemore, who had identified himself as the head of the personnel department of a research laboratory at Rockville, Maryland; sat to the right of commercial artist Clyde Warmack, a slender, grey haired gentleman with a wide, stern mouth and large Adam's apple. Mr. Sizemore said that Mr. Warmack was from the small Maryland town of Poolesville, a town near the laboratory. Sizemore listed himself as a Virginian from Roanoke. The janitor of the laboratory where the men worked, with serious, unsmiling face, with eyes on the worn and patched macadam road, drives the Dodge.

The car sped forward through the early afternoon. "Every few miles more we travel through these wastes of fields and trees, I imagine another person in the car with us. There must be fifteen or sixteen in here now. Hubert, there had better be some fish in that water."

"Oh, there're fish in there, Dr. Kavanagh," said Hubert, his hands on the wheel, his eyes on the brown MacAdam Road that stretched out in front of him.

"Owen, I don't know where you're putting all these extra people you're filling our car with. As I see it, we aren't going all the way into that wilderness because of a great quantity of fish. We are going for the experience of fishing in a time-honoured way, in surroundings barely disturbed by man, as man has dovetailed into, become part of the nature he invades. For a brief space of time, we will join that

16

portion of mankind who continue in that ancient vocation of fishing for a living; then, prepare and eat food we ourselves have obtained. Eat fish fried over a driftwood fire, feel the wet winds off the water, listen to the river's flow, watch the many-coloured flames glowing out of gnarled driftwood."

"You make it sound very romantic, Donald," said Dr. Kavanagh. "I only said, when I go fishing, I like to catch fish. That's all."

Donald Fleckenstein sat looking out the other window in the back seat of Hubert Stokes' old box-like Dodge. He said, "If we were going only for the pleasure of pulling fish out of the water on a baited hook, we should have headed for that artificial lake at Columbia. We would have been there by now. We would be sitting on sand trucked in from some place, under a concrete beach umbrella. For scenery we would have had a ten foot plastic Indian, squatted over a plastic campfire, to gaze at. But we would have pulled in a shitload of the most handsome bass and bream, or we would have complained to the management, complained so loud that we would have been given an extra two hours, free of charge, during which time the manager's son would have swam under the water, put fish on our hooks. Then a tank truck would have been up from the fisheries first thing Monday, made sure nobody would holler next week end."

"You know none of us are in that bag, Donald," said Dr. Kavanagh from the other side of the car.

Mr. Sizemore looked back from his front seat. "Owen is just scared he won't get to eat anything tomorrow. The rest of us, we don't catch anything, can eat our sausage and bread. Owen, being Catholic, tomorrow being Friday, Owen will catch fish or starve."

"I'm not Catholic. Why, Hell no. My mother and father were church-goers, though; so, were socially part of the Catholic community, but don't think for a minute that I, since I've been old enough to add two and two, ever believed in Jesus Christ, the virginity of his mother and such," said Dr. Kavanagh.

"Well, I'd taken it for granted none of you scientists believed in God. I've heard tell all scientists were atheists," said Hubert.

Dr. Flytell, a tall, thin, serious-looking man, long nose on a thin face, frizzly electric hair standing up on his head, sat next to Dr. Kavanagh. "I think that statement, generally speaking, describes the situation. I think most scientists could be classifiable as basically atheist," he said.

"I just don't think that's true," said Dr. Fleckenstein. "Rebelling against the Catholic upbringing of my childhood, in college, I fancied myself an atheist; but with a less emotional look at what might be termed theological considerations, I find so many questions on which we all must say, we aren't sure; that, in spite of how we answer question after question individually, we must all accept classification as one shade or another of agnostic."

"My grandfather seldom used the term agnostic," said Dr. Fogwell, a trim, gray-haired man seated between Dr. Flytell and Dr. Fleckenstein. "For any man who couldn't see the obvious validity of the Bible, he preferred the Latin equivalent to agnostic, which is ignoramus."

"Every man must be some mixture of believer and doubter," said Mr. Warmack, a slender man with dark hair and spectacles, seated between Mr. Sizemore and the driver, "but a basic belief in God seems logical. I wouldn't want to be termed an agnostic because I have some doubts and reservations. I don't believe everything my parson tells me, but I believe in God."

"Being an artist," said Dr. Flytell, "I would have thought you'd be a Zen Buddhist or something."

"He is a commercial artist, Estel," said Mr. Sizemore, "which in a way makes him more of a scientist than any of you doctors in physics. Besides, I suspect there are no Zen Buddhists in Poolesville, Maryland."

"None that I know of," said Mr. Warmack.

"I would think it more likely that Donald here is more the Zen Buddhist artist type. Look at his beard," said Mr. Sizemore.

"Zen has much to recommend it," said Dr. Fleckenstein.

"In spite of being able to prove very little," said Dr. Fogwell, "I think that we all can find something we can believe in. There are points in many of the philosophies of life, of death, in which we see some rightness. One philosophy I find refutable though, is that of atheism. I don't believe any of us could be completely an atheist, could believe in no possibility of the existence of any power which could be termed God, in no possibility for our extension, in any way, into eternity."

"I'm an atheist," said Dr. Flytell. "Henry, I don't believe in anything. Not Jesus Christ, nor Buddha, nor Zoroaster, nor Odin, nor Ra, nor Pan, nor Saturn, nor Janus, nor Jupiter, nor Jove, nor Koronos, Caos, King Arthur. I don't even believe in Santa Klaus."

The car drove on in silence over a road darkened by the trees which lined either side. Through a break in the trees to the right, the red sun could be seen low over the brush-covered wastes. Now a tunnel of trees. Now marsh grass and water to the right, to the left, to the left and right. Now more woods. The sun had set and the car turned onto a bumpy dirt road, into the middle of tall trees. The car stopped. The men climbed out. Hubert went to a trunk attached to the back of his car, got out sleeping bags, fishing gear, a box containing food.

"Get a fire going before it gets too dark to see," said Hubert. "I thought that was in your line," said Dr. Kavanagh.

"You needing it made in the middle of your laboratory, and it would be," said Hubert, "but there's no janitors here. Tables is turned. Least, we are just seven fisher men needing a fire. Come on, let's get a good spot, then put our bags where we want to sleep. It's nice and dry here and we're just a short walk to the water, and down to Townshend's Landing where we can rent out boats."

Mr. Warmack and Mr. Sizemore had gathered rocks and were setting the location for the fire. The others began gathering wood and putting it at the location. In now what was the dark, Mr. Warmack started a fire going. Hubert brought over the box of food and a grill, put the grill by the fire, leaning against the rocks. The fire blazed up, lit up the ground a little ways between the dark trees. The fire burned lower. The men stood around and watched.

"This feels something like the woods around the Potomac, except for the sound. The Potomac at Poolesville is a loud river. It has the rapids at Violets Lock. You can hear 'em a mile away," said Mr. Warmack.

"This feels somewhat like back home," said Dr. Fogwell, "except it has a more remote, wilder feel."

The sound of the water was perceptible. Somewhere, the swish against the shores. The fire burned low. Hubert put the grill on the rocks over the fire, got out hot dogs, put seven of them on the grill. The others stood and watched. Dr. Fleckenstein turned them over with a long-handled fork, watched as the grease dripped down, sizzled and blazed against the low flames. He got a roll, speared a hot dog, put it in the roll, handed it to Mr. Sizemore, fixed another, and handed it to Dr. Flytell. He fixed one, handed it to Dr. Fogwell. Hubert got the ketchup, put some on his hot dog, passed the ketchup to Dr. Fogwell. The men ate.

"Put on some more?" asked Mr. Sizemore.

"Yes," said Dr. Flytell. "Let's have another round."

Mr. Sizemore lined up another row of hot dogs across the grill. The wind came up, sighed in the tops of the trees. The tops bent in the wind.

"This is sort of spooky," said Dr. Flytell.

"Don't tell me a good atheist, like yourself, believes in spooks," said Dr. Fleckenstein.

"I don't. I don't, but I'm not used to all this wild outdoors. I'm more used to well-run parks. You men are more outdoorsmen than I am. Even you and Kavanagh: you with your picnics all around the Maryland and Vrrginia countryside; Kavanagh with his vacations in Maine. Listen to that wind."

The wind, in answer, whistled and bent the tops of the trees. Dr. Fogwell took the fork, turned the hot dogs. The grease spat against the red coals. The darkness had closed in on the circle of men. Reflections off the ruby coals glinted off the men's faces; off, here and there, parts of their wearing apparel; buckles, buttons glittered in the orange light.

"It doesn't seem anybody would live within miles of here, Hubert," said Dr.

Kavanagh.

"I live up in Trappe, on the river about five miles up," said Hubert.

The men stood in silence. Only the wind was loud in the tops of the trees. The tree tops bent back and forth.

Dr. Kavanagh got the fork, took the hot dogs off the grill, put one in a roll, handed it to Dr. Fogwell, and put another in a roll. Hubert got the catsup, put some on his hot dog, handed the catsup to Dr. Fogwell and bit his hot dog. The men ate. Hubert wiped his hands on his pants, took a stick and pulled the grill off the coals. Dr.

Fleckenstein and Mr. Sizemore drug sleeping bags over, looked at them in the dimming light.

"Here's yours, Henry," said Mr. Sizemore. Mr. Warmack got his sleeping bag from the back of the car. Hubert got his and brought a shovel around from the trunk of the car.

"There's a flashlight and toilet paper in the box here. The shovel will be beside it," he said. He took the short-handled shovel, scooped up dirt, put it on the coals.

"Pleasant dreams, everybody," he said. He took his sleeping bag, felt out a level place, spread it out. The wind sighed through the trees, was still.

Hubert shook a form in the darkness, the flashlight making a bright path into the trees.

"Come on, time to rise or the sun will catch us still in the sack." "Huh? Huh? What time is it?" said the voice of Dr. Kavanagh. "It's quarter till four," said Hubert.

Dr. Kavanagh sat up. The others started stirring, getting up. They rolled their sacks, took them to the car, got their fishing rods, and tackle boxes.

"Follow me," said Hubert. His flashlight beam marked a path through the trees. The men stumbled behind it, down a slope, over a fallen log, through some low brush, out on the sandy banks of a body of water. Pale mist hung over the water.

The flashlight turned, flashed over everybody, turned to the left. The men walked over driftwood and root-covered flats. The water bent in and the men turned to the left. In the distance flickered a light. The men walked towards that. The beam of the flashlight walked in front of them, shone into rising mists. In front of them was an old shack. Hubert walked up to the door.

"Mr. Townshend," he called.

"Who's there?" came a man's voice from inside. Light flickered out of a little window to the right of the door.

"It's me, Hubert Stokes."

The door unbolted, sagged open.

"That you, Hubert?", said the wrinkled, gray-haired man standing in the doorway. To the right, an old pier went out into the water. The end of it stuck out, hidden in the mists. Near the shore, some posts stuck out of the water. Out in the mist, a small, squat, two-mast sailboat, a bug eye, was moored.

"We want to rent some boats," said Hubert.

"You gone plumb daft, Hubert?", said the old man. "Why? Oh my gosh. It's Mermaid Day," said Hubert.

"That's right, and your friends can't be from here 'bouts, else they're feeling mighty hardy, can't much value their lives. But I noways took you for a man that was cracked in the head, Hubert. But I can't be rentin' out boats till after sunrise. Can't afford to get any lost."

"What do we do now?", said Hubert.

My advice; go down on the beach, make a big fire, wait till sunrise. Else join Hambrick down the beach a way. He's waitin' till after sunrise to take his boat out.

That's it tied up there" He closed and bolted his door.

"Come on, hurry," said Hubert. He went quickly around the shack, down along the water toward a fire which glowed a few hundred yards down the beach. They got closer. They could see four men standing around a blazing fire. The men walked up to it.

"Hello, Merrill," said Hubert as the men walked up.

"Hubert. I didn't expect to see anybody near the water today. Thought everybody'd be in their homes with their doors and windows locked. Who you got with you?"

"Tell you, I clean forgot about it being Mermaid Day," said Hubert. "These are my friends; Dr. Kavanagh, Dr. Flytell, Mr. Sizemore, Dr. Fogwell, Dr. Fleckenstein and Mr. Warmack. Men - these are my fellow townsmen: Merrill Hambrick, Otis Whitcomb, Evan Shuffel

22

and John Barnes."

"Glad to have you with us. It's a good morning to have lots of company," said Merrill. "Even with these guns here, we almost stayed in our homes. But it's hard to miss a day's fishing. It's our livelihood."

Each of the men had the muzzle of a shotgun in his hand. Somewhere, a mournful ailp ailp. The men jumped.

"Just a loon," said Merrill.

"Man, that's a weird sound," said Dr. Flytell.

"I know people as heard them all they's lives, hears one, goes in search of the drownin' woman," said Merrill.

"Swears he hears her despairin' help help as she goes down the third time," said Evan.

Mist rose in the low places below where the men stood.

"You men aren't from 'round here. You down from Salisbury or somewheres?" Otis asked.

"We've come over from Washington," said Mr. Sizemore. "I'm from Baltimore," said Dr. Fleckenstein.

"Not many get down here from Baltimore," said John.

"I'm from Charleston, South Carolina," said Dr. Fogwell. "Everett, here, is from Roanoke; Clyde from Poolesville on the Potomac, Estel from New York, and Owen from Boston. But we are all taking time off from the Federal Patent Research Laboratory near Washington."

The mist flooded in about their feet. Somewhere, a gull squawked. They listened.

"Then you all are scientists?", said Evan.

"Four of us," said Dr. Fogwell. "Everett is head of the Personnel Department.

Clyde does our art work, illustrates our reports."

Wisps of mist blew over the water. The wood in the fire fell, sending up sparks, burned lower.

"You know," said Dr. Kavanagh, "if there be any truth in the tales I'm told of mermaids, those guns will be of no help."

"Now don't tell me you believe in mermaids, Owen," said Dr. Flytell. "You've reasoned away the Catholic Church, but not the tons of other superstitions your Irish ancestors bandied about. Come on, Owen, there are no mermaids."

"Believing in life and eternity, as presented by the Bible; believing in the many other strange, seemingly otherworldly phenomena; these are two different things entirely. Accounts and sightings of mermaids are a whole lot better documented than Jesus Christ rising from the dead," said Dr. Kavanagh.

"Mr. Gebbehardy, the parson in town, says belief in mermaids is unholy. He says there ain't no mermaids," said Evan.

"Then why ain't he out there fishin'?", said John.

"But you're right, Doc," said Merrill. "We know you can't shoot mermaids. We just feel safer with them guns than without. Actually, we'd just make a lot of noise with them, hope the mermaids would go away."

There was a noise up the beach. The men jumped, picked up their guns. Two shapes were coming toward them.

"Hello there," said a voice.

"There, tis only Doc Nuttle, our sawbones," said Merrill. "Hello, Doc."

Two men were coming up, carrying fishing gear. The man to the rear carried, besides his fishing rod, a large pistol. The man in front spoke.

"I get a day off rarely enough, I'm not letting any mermaids drive me off from the little pleasure I get. I get here and I can't even rent a boat. This is Cobby Perkins, from over at Pocomoke City. I told him that horse pistol would do him no good. If we see mermaids, just better start praying to God Almighty."

"Six to one, half a dozen to the other, as far as shooting and praying go. I'm Owen Kavanagh, over from the Federal Patents Research Laboratory near Washington. Actually, it's at Rockville. This is Clyde Warmack, Everett Sizemore, Henry Fogwell, Donald Fleckenstein and Estel Flytell. Hubert works there, and we came over with him."

"I'm Neil Nuttle. Titis is Cobby Perkins. I couldn't find anybody from Trappe to come fishing with me. And I asked a dozen or more before I gave it up and called Cobby in Pocomoke. And I had to twist his arm. I thought I was going to have to bring down somebody from back home. I'm from up at Cambridge."

"That's Cambridge, Maryland, Owen," said Dr. Fleckenstein.

The waves slapped the shore below them. The mist moved across the water. "You're a brave man, Doc," said Merrill. "Gonna wrestle mermaids! You gonna help the doc wrestle mermaids, Cobby?" "No, I ain't," said Cobby Perkins.

"You ain't? And the doc been teaching you arm twistin'," said Merrill. "The doc ain't teachin' me no arm twistin'," said Cobby.

"Tell me, Dr. Kavanagh," said Otis. "Wasn't it pretty hard, an awful feeling, for your folks to have got to Boston an' had all them Yankees everywhere?"

"Aw, Otis, Dr. Kavanagh, he is a Yankee," said John.

Otis objected. "Not really. He's an Irishman. I bet his folks was all over in Ireland when all them Yankees invaded the South."

"You mean, like coming over here with the likes of Flytell?," said Dr. Kavanagh.

"No, he doesn't look like a Yankee," said Otis. "He looks different from anything, an' I've seen Yankees. If Dr. Flytell were introduced as The Man in the Moon, I wouldn't much doubt it. I wouldn't call no one no liar for saying it!"

"Now, I've been up the shore, visiting my cousin; that's Chestertown. I've seen Yankees there. My cousin told me they bought a place on the river there, then all the folk as lived there all their lives couldn't go near the place. Only them and friends that come to see them from Pennsylvania."

"If the Mayor of Phaldelphey was standin' here, I couldn't find nothin' good to say 'bout Pennsylvania," said Evan.

Dr. Kavanagh explained to Otis, "It's true, many of my folks were in Ireland when the Civil War was fought. My father came to this country as a small boy. My mother's father, in about 1880. However, mother's mother was a Lowell and, of course, a Yankee."

"My folks always spoke well of the Lowells," said Mr. Warmack.

"Yeah. If one has to be a Yankee, Owen, a Lowell is the best kind," said Dr. Fogwell, laughing.

"So, Flytell, you're the Man in the Moon," said Mr. Sizemore. "Estel's something he doesn't even believe in."

"That may be true," said Dr. Fleckenstein. "I'm interested in these mermaids.

I saw something in the newspaper back home about them, some column called 'Our Backwoods Oddities', but I forget what I read."

There were pale lemon streaks in the sky toward the East. Mist swirled over the water and in the low gullies around them.

"Well," said Merrill, "all I know is way back they used to honor the mermaids like they was holy angels. They used to leave the most beautiful girls on the beach, and the mermaids would select the one most beautiful. By the time the sun rose, she was gone. Then, sometimes they'd see her swimming in the water, so they'd know she was a beautiful mermaid. Then a preacher came and said they was worshipping the Devil, that they couldn't do it no more. They stopped sending girls to the beaches. But, people still kept disappearing on Mermaid Day. On account of the preachers, people started getting scared of the mermaids, locking themselves in their houses. Then not only beautiful girls started disappearing, sometimes old ladies; sometimes, even mens."

"There's caves below here a ways, near the coast, where at high tides the water tinkles and falls over the rocks like bells. People call it Mermaid Caves, and folks stay away from there," said Evan.

Otis said, "Do you really believe in mermaids? The preacher says they ain't any such things. They's against the Bible."

"Oh, they's mermaids, all right," said Merrill.

"I don't know. They may be just make believe stories, but somebody, Old Mrs. Fenwick, did disappear some years ago. And it was Mermaids Day," said John. "Then, before that, that fisherman disappeared," Evan said.

"But this isn't every Mermaid Day," said Hubert. "It was nine years ago Old Lady Fenwick disappeared. Then, the next year, nobody stayed inside or locked any doors. They had a flower festival, which the parson criticized, you remember."

"That's right. It's only every ninth Mermaid Day, of course, scares people, not just Mermaid Day. This is the ninth year Mermaid Day," said Merrill.

"That's right, we don't act like this every year," said John.

"This is givin' me the creeps, an' I don't mind tellin' you," said Cobby. He stood and shivered in the damp silence.

"Maybe we should go home," said Mr. Warmack. "Yeah, let's all get out of here," said Cobby.

"And walk through them dark woods? Suit yourself. I mean, mermaids or no, them woods is spooky," said Otis. "an' it's not so dark here. And there's the fire."

The eastern sky was yellow with pale pink in it. Mist swirled off the water, billowed up around them. Evan put more wood on the fire. It blazed up.

"If you gentlemen will excuse me, I've got to go take a shit some place. Hand me that little old shovel, Hubert. Now, that roll of toilet paper out of your box, Owen," said Dr. Flytell.

"Man, wait till after sunrise," said Merrill. "It's not a long wait. The sun'll be up directly. Look at that East. See them orangy clouds down near the water. Man, wait."

"I sorta like the nice darkness for shitting in," said Dr. Flytell.

"Man, who would see you on Mermaid Day? All the women's locked in their houses," said Evan.

"Well, hand me that shovel."

"Maybe I should go with you with a gun," said Hubert. "But I don't trust guns with mermaids. I wish you'd wait."

"Shit, no," said Dr. Flytell. "And I don't need you with any gun to help me shit either. See you gents in a minute."

"Frankly, I don't believe the mermaid story," said Dr. Nuttle, "but I wouldn't be wanderin' off about now. Strange things happen in this world."

"If they're after beautiful girls, Fly's safe enough," said Dr. Fogwell.

"Old Lady Fenwick warn't no beautiful girl," said Evan. "Old Avery warn't neither."

The clouds in the east got golden, tinged with bright orange. Lakes of mist floated in off the water, covered the men, floated away. "Did you hear that," said John.

Everybody listened. A couple of gulls cackled somewhere. There was a gargling sound. Everybody jumped.

"It's only the waves playing tricks on us," said Otis. "There it is," hollered Evan.

"No, that's Flytell," said Dr. Fleckenstein.

The head of Dr. Flytell floated toward them over a pool of mist.

"I admit it looks spooky," said Dr. Fogwell. "You see a head, no body." The head came toward them, over the lake of pale mist, passed them by, looking neither right nor left, and floated out toward the sea.

"That's funny," said Dr. Fleckenstein. "Over here, Fly. Over here," he hollered.

The head floated on toward the sea. The mist swirled away.

"Holy Mother of God," said Dr. Kavanagh. He crossed himself.

"It's horrible," said Mr. Sizemore.

"The others stood and stared. It sunk into the mist above the water. The sun came up. The men looked all around, walking through the bushes.

"Look here," said Mr. Warmack.

The men, one by one, came over. There was a little shovel, a hole, all splashed with blood. Blood on sticks, on leaves, on everything.

"Horrible," said Otis.

Dr. Fleckenstein, Dr. Fogwell, Dr. Kavanagh, Mr. Sizemore, and Mr. Warmack started down the beach.

"Come, Hubert," said Dr. Fleckenstein. "Poor Fly," said Dr. Kavanagh

"Yes," said Dr. Fogwell. "Well, perhaps at last Flytell found something he can believe in."

"That's dreadful, Henry," said Dr. Fleckenstein.

About fifteen years after I wrote "Mermaids of Nanticoke", a newspaper article appeared, an article by John Buettner, which suggested that my story might contain within it a grain of truth. The article asked, "Who knows what creatures wallow in the ooze and the slime of the Chesapeake and the waterways which empty into it." Sightings were listed for spooky creatures, with names like Nessie, Chessie, and Champ. Some of the reports have come out of the Native American past. John Buettner's article appeared in *The Elm,* February 28, 1986.

Too Much Green

I got to the town where I expected to find a hotel, but before I saw the hotel, I saw an art gallery. I parked, went in to take a look. As I walked in, the curator, from his office, spotted me. He came out.

"Ah Tom, surprise. Let me show you around the gallery, then we'll have a drink and talk about them."

He was holding a glass of wine as he spoke. His deep voice rumbled, as we walked along, to explain points of interest of one picture after another. Here, the water in a brook was of particular interest. The large, stout and greying art critic moved on to the next picture. He opened his wide mouth, his deep voice rumbled, rolled out, "Now here is a Worthington. In the tradition of Constable."

"I rather like it," I said.

"All well enough in concept. In concept," said the curator, "And had he handled his colours tastefully. And it might have been quite good. But look at this, this vulgar green botched into everything.,"

He waved his glass, his drink spilling.

"Green, green. Look at it. Hideous green all over the God damned picture." He was shaking his glass back and forth so that the drink slushed out.

"Just look at it," he thundered, "Green, green, green, green everyplace." He looked, noticed his drink was spilling, turned his glass upside down. "Green," he thundered, throwing the glass on the floor.

There was a great crash.

The security guard came from around a corner. "Is there a problem, Dr. Humphries?"

"No, I was explaining to Tom, here, this picture. contains too much green." The officer went up and looked at the picture, looked at it all over.

"I would have to think about it," he said.

"Well, I'm not going through the whole explanation all over again," the curator emphatically stated.

"But do you need to be so loud about it?"

"It's a LOUD PICTURE."

The officer walked toward the door.

"And Officer, tell William to give us a bit of a clean up, if you would please."

I suspect what had annoyed Dr. Humphries was that I hadn't seemed to observe that the green should have been tastefully suggested in a way which would have demonstrated good craftsmanship. I'm certain I got no better than a D minus on that exam.

Holding On

Holding On

Bill heard a step in the hall, heard the mailbox rattle. He stopped ironing a shirt, went to see what piece of mail might have arrived. It was a wedding invitation. It was from his girlfriend of long past; from his years 13 through 15. He had been sure he had found love eternal and Lynn, he was certain, had felt the same. Life, however, is not constructed solely of spirit: there is the continuing need of addressing problems in the physical world. One can be in love, yet be unprepared for combating, with any measure of success, the problems that would be manifested by permitting love to lead to marriage. Bill told himself he wanted Lynn to have, in her adult years, a nice home and economic advantages for her children, especially since she had had these economic advantages in her young years. And Bill seemed unable to find a job that would supply these things.

Now, when Bill thought of Lynn, he told himself he hoped she would marry someone who could afford a nice home, but he wasn't prepared for a wedding invita tion. Suddenly, he wanted to be far away. Bill got satchels and suitcases from his closets, packed clothes he wanted to take, put a selection of books in boxes, wrapped and tied the pictures from his walls. Then the little things - a big box for odds and ends; then, packing his car, a small marble top stand would fit in and too, a wooden chair.

Then he put, in the remaining space on his back seat, dishes, pots, pans and sacks of food. He got a few more books and filled empty spaces in the car trunk, in the space between the front and back seat. He'd packed enough. It was time to go.

"Now for my farewell supper," Bill stated aloud for his own ears. He cooked himself sausage and eggs, ate, and quickly rinsed the pan. He made one quick check of his apartment for anything he might have overlooked, then drove off. He drove, in a leisurely way, up a shady back road.

"There is sure no hurry," he told himself. "There's no one waiting at the end of the world for Bill."

Bill drove over the old river bridge, wound in and out of the back roads in a run down section of town, then he was driving through the country, driving along twisty country roads. The late spring dusk was fading to darkness. Dark shadows of trees crossed the road. At a shaded crossroads, a shadowy shape looked like a woman. It was a woman in a dark cape and hood. The shadow flagged him down, got in. Bill drove on, drove in silence

Bill glanced at his companion. Concealed in shadow as she seemed, he yet could tell she was young and scantily clad, a young girl.

"Where you going?" she asked.

"To the end of the world." Bill drove on down the dark road. "Where are you going?"

"To the end of the world." Her voice was almost a whisper. Bill took a better look.

It seemed she wore but a filmy white nightgown under her cape.

"Lynn??"

She turned and faced him.

"But you're getting married Wednesday."

"Am I?" A trace of smile touched her lips.

Bill drove on. He glanced at the girl beside him. It was Lynn.

"I went to your place to be sure you'd be - but you were gone, and I realized neither of us could just go forward without -"

Bill glanced over, caught Lynn's eye. They smiled. Bill drove on through the dark, drove through a small dark town, out under a star-covered sky, through another small town. Then the lights of a larger town were in front of them.

"Are you going to drive all night?" "Well, I'd thought to stop - ."

"You could stop at a motel. It's a long way to the end of the world."

"No, we can't make it non-stop, can we?" Bill pulled in at a motel. It was still a good way to the lights of town. Bill went to the office, got the key to a cabin, hurried back to the car. Lynn was still there. He helped her out of the car; then, as they walked, Lynn told Bill, "Do things right, now. Carry me over the threshold."

"But we haven't had our wedding."

"I'd rather not think of weddings for awhile. That word makes me sad. I don't think Adam and Eve had one. Not with all the trappings, anyway."

Bill carried Lynn into the cabin, found a light and turned it on. Bill went back for a satchel and a small sack of food. When he got back, Lynn was in bed.

"I can't eat a thing tonight, Bill."

Bill made a sandwich, ate it, then took some things from his satchel and went to wash. He spread lather on his face.

"Come on, Bill. This is our night. The earth and the sky and the seas are waiting for us to be happy."

"Happy? What on earth could all of them be waiting for?"

"Then there's no rush," she said, as Bill climbed into bed. Bill, running his fingers gently over Lynn's shoulder and back, asked "Could you be more happy?"

Lynn lay silent for a few seconds. "I have a full cup; but for happiness, I don't think you'd find a measuring cup. And perhaps the most intense happiness is set in a frame of tears. I cried when your car stopped. You didn't notice?"

"It was dark, but our tears are gone now; our dark, lonesome nights have passed, and here we are together. It had to be."

In the morning Bill awoke. Lynn lay beside him, the picture of peace. He touched her hair.

"I knew you'd be beside me someday." She opened her eyes, smiled.

Said Bill, "I'll say, in the morning light, you look solid enough."

Lynn sat up. "I think I'll order buttered toast and orange juice. You'll need to bring them to me, as I doubt that you have anything that would fit me."

"Then off I go. No coffee?" "No coffee."

Bill was soon back with their breakfast, coffee for himself. They ate in silence. Bill got up and washed. Lynn called, "Would you run into town, buy me a shirt, jeans and sandals? I've written down the sizes."

Bill took the paper, drove off. Soon he was back. "I wish you'd been with me to select."

"No need. You did fine." Lynn took off her nightgown and put on the shirt and jeans, "Let's be off."

After turning in the key, they drove into town. They came to a department store. "Let's stop," said Lynn.

They parked and went in. Lynn led Bill around, bought herself some clothes.

"O.K., let's go," she said.

Out in the country, they had sandwiches for lunch; then, drove till past sundown; then drove to a motel where they might have supper and a room for the night. In the motel lobby, Lynn stopped in front of a rack of postcards, selected one, went to a stamp machine and got a stamp. She wrote on the card, read it to Bill: "I'm happy and send love to you both."

She saw a tall gentleman discussing postcards with his wife. "Where are you bound for?" asked Lynn.

"Hattisburg. Going home."

"May I give you a card to mail from Hattisburg?" "You sure can."

Lynn gave him the card. She and Bill went to their room. Bill was especially gentle. He couldn't free himself of the notion that Lynn was fragile, his impression from when he saw her at the crossroads; how she seemed then, created of unsubstantial shadow. The next morning, Bill and Lynn returned to the road, traveled together through the days of early summer until they came to Brownsville. While they were stopped here, Lynn got herself a job as a waitress.

Then it was Thursday, Lynn's off day. Bill and Lynn drove around, looked at flats, rented the most economical one they could find. Bill fixed it up between searching for a job for himself. He looked at two help wanted ads. Lynn came in from work.

"Look, Lynn, two help wanteds. One, Jack's Entrenching Company; then, here, Grand Prize Hardware."

"I like the hardware," said Lynn. "First, there are construction accidents. If anything happens to you, we're high and dry. A bit of news. I'm pregnant."

"Wow! Must have been that first night. That's for sure?"

"I checked at the doctor's before work."

"Then we should get champagne."

"No alcohol for me. I'm going to do everything right. We'll need a good name. All its own. Be thinking."

"Wow, what news. I think I'll try for both jobs. The digging, you report way early a.m. Getting there at that hour is half the battle. If I fail to land that, I'll come home, get a tie."

"Too bad you can't put the tie on first."

"Wouldn't the other workers laugh, digging ditches wearing a tie. You never can tell, though. It might land me the job."

In a happy mood, they prepared supper for themselves. After supper, Bill laid out clothes for himself, went to bed early. Then the alarm went off. Bill got right up.

Slightly overdressed in a western hat and string tie, he kissed Lynn and left.

By lunch time, Bill thought he'd dug ditches enough to stretch half way across the state. At the end of the day, the boss said, "See you tomorrow, young feller."

That evening, he and Lynn were tired but happy. The next day, sore as he was, Bill was back on the job giving those ditches his best. The days went on. Digging got easier for him and he tried to learn as much as he could about ditches. After work, Bill picked up Lynn at her work. He was glad to observe she was very popular there.

"You know, Bill, I could get you a job here," she said.

"There would be disadvantages in the two of us working in the same place," said Bill.

"I thought of that. But I'm sure you'd master any difficulties."

"But I'm doing well where I am. The boss is teaching me about the blueprints. When he's not there, I can keep the job going. I think it's better to have money coming in from two different places."

"I suppose so," said Lynn.

Weeks passed. The summer faded into autumn. Lynn was noticeably pregnant. It was late October.

Lynn said, "Oh, Bill, I can't work any more." Tears ran down her face. "It seems foolish at this stage, but I'm a bit scared of this. I want the baby so much, but I can sense trouble."

"This is our first," said Bill. "We want it as easy and safe as we and science can make it."

Lynn called her work, went to a doctor, had a physical. The doctor called Bill. "Lynn isn't any too strong, seems to have once been involved in an accident; but if all goes well, we might let her have her baby. She's to be careful. No falls."

Bill was determined Lynn was going to be careful. Then it was Christmas season. Bill, when he wasn't working, hardly let Lynn out of his sight. Bill and Lynn sent a card to her mother and father, but no other cards. Bill decorated a tree and, together, they listened to Christmas music. Lynn seemed very tired much of the time. January came. The doctor said it might be best to get the baby. Then the baby was born, a boy.

"I'm so happy," said Lynn.

"I'm on Cloud Nine," said Bill. "Isn't he just marvelous? Just look at him." Bill put his cheek on Lynn's hair. Said Lynn, "We should call Mom and Pop."

Bill and the doctor smiled and shook hands. Then Bill and Lynn called Mom and Pop. Lynn's mother picked up the phone.

"Hello, Mom, it's Lynn. I have a baby!"

"Hello, hello, who? I can't hear." Bill took the phone. "This is Bill. We have a baby boy."

"Oh, Bill, I'm so glad. We were wondering, it had been so long. It's so nice of you to think of us. Congratulations."

Lynn took the phone. "Mom, this is Lynn. This is Lynn."

"Bill, sorry I have to run. I think I hear Lynn calling." She hung up.

"I wonder if she thought you weren't on the phone?"

"Well, I don't know," said Lynn.

Lynn seemed slow regaining her strength, but Bill was so full of energy, he was glad for Lynn to lay quiet most of the time. The days passed, spring came and went and summer. Then another fall. Christmas was quiet but joyful. Bill and Lynn had a son to buy things for. They had a bright tree and kept Christmas music playing. Then January. It was their son's birthday. Bill lit the candle on a small cake. The three of them blew it out. As the blown out candle smoked, Lynn said,

"We need to go home. I'll see Mom and Pop and they'll want to see Michael." "And we can tell them we're doing pretty well. They should be glad to hear."

"When do you want to go?"

"Right now. As soon as we can pack."

Bill called his job. In two hours they were on the road. They drove nearly non stop. Lynn seemed always ready to push on. Then, on an evening, the car pulled up in the large, shady yard of Lynn's mom and pop. Now they were there, Lynn seemed pale and shaky.

"You go up first. Tell them I've come home. I can't do it yet."

"It's all right, Lynn. They'll love to have you. If not, we are with each other with a love like fire."

Bill turned and went to the front door. Lynn's brother opened it. "Bill, what a surprise. I'll get Mom and Pop."

An elderly man came, shook Bill's hand, ushered him inside. "I've brought your daughter home."

"What? Our daughter's here."

"Yes, outside."

"No, she's upstairs."

"Well, I left her out at the car."

"You must have been imagining. You mean Lynn? She's been up in her bed for better than half a year."

"But she's been a waitress in Brownsville."

"It must have been some other Lynn. Our Lynn, you didn't hear. She jumped off the river bridge. They brought her home. Been in and out of consciousness ever since. I'm afraid she's slipping away now, but I'm glad you've come. She's been asking for you the past couple of days. Come."

Pop led Bill upstairs to a bedroom. There was Lynn, pale and broken on her bed. "Bill?" said Lynn.

"Lynn. I don't understand." He took her hand.

"Bill, I think I can come in now."

Bill let go her hand, rushed downstairs and out to the car. Lynn was leaning on the car. She started toward him to meet him. But then the dress fell to the ground and she was nothing but cloud. Bill ran to the car. His son reached for him, but then he too was mist. His clothes fell limp to the seat of the car. Pop came out, picked up his daughter's dress.

"Her choice of a dress is what we'd want."

"But the card from Hattisburg," said Bill. "You knew about that."

"We took that as a last goodbye. We never knew how she got to Hattisburg, or when she wrote it."

A Drive In the Country

The car made its way down the worn country road. Just yesterday afternoon, the driver had been at his desk trying to rewrite some reports. Then he pushed the papers away, said to himself, "To Hell with all of this. I'm on vacation this week. What am I doing this now for? Think I'll take a drive."

He put on his jacket, walked out to his car and was on the road. The road took him to Richmond. There he spent the night. Then, instead of returning to Falls Church, where he lived, he had decided to drive around the countryside. Much of the day had passed and he was still driving around the countryside. Now and again, trees threw their shadows across the road.

The blue mountains in front had begun to change colour, to dark blued greens.

Above them, white fleecy clouds sailed through the blue. The worn macadam road, through tall weeds and brambles, which bordered here green rocky fields; bent to the right, bent to the left. To the right, a yellowish house and dilapidated grey barn came into view a few fields over from the road. The road rose up, curved to the right, and sank into a wooded valley. Houses of stone and wood stood close to either side of the road which leapt down a steep slope, bent sharply in a curve to the right, ended at a creek, at a broken stone bridge around which the water gushed madly. The water was flooding high into the bushy green banks. On the other side of the creek, the road climbed up into a wooded hill. On the right, on a ridge over the creek, were the backs of buildings. Their crumbling, worn stone foundations sank down toward the water. An officer, wide brimmed hat, trim brown uniform, walked up.

"Are you Dr. Baliles?"

"Yes. Yes. How did you know?"

"Come with me, if you please, sir," said the officer.

"Because I'm on vacation, just decided to take a long drive. This is a

A Drive in the Country

long way from Falls Church, my home. Spent the night in Richmond. This is a long way from Richmond. I had lunch at gosh knows where. And where is this? How did you know my name is Baliles?"

"This way sir," said the officer.

The officer led the way down a path by the creek, around some rocky cliffs. Then here was a square building of old reddish grey stones. Small windows faced the front. A low doorway led into a narrow, dark hallway; that, to a largish room lit by dull yellow globes which hung from the ceiling. The room was filled with wooden pews and these, filled with people. A thin man with grey hair entered from the front. He wore a dark suit. "Will the court please rise," he said.

Everybody stood up. A tall, big shouldered man entered. A mound of silver white hair he had, over a long, pleasant face. Bushy white eyebrows were over his steel blue eyes. The judge took his place.

"The case of Albion Baliles versus the City of Waterford," said the judge, the light glinting off his rimless spectacles.

Seeming younger than his white hair would indicate he was, the judge smiled at everybody. The court was silent. Only in the back comer, a tall, thin man stood rattling his notes. His hair was steel grey and curly and in long side whiskers, extended beyond his ears.

There were whispers in the court. The shuffling sound of the papers continued.

"Mr. Whistler," the judge was speaking to the man in the comer, "is your client in the court?"

The man spoken to raised his long arm and, with his bony finger, pointed.

"Mr. Applegate, have you your case prepared?"

"I have, your honour," said a big, stoutish man.

Mr. Applegate looked over at the defendant. He put his horn rimmed spectacles on his squarish face so he could look at the defendant better.

Said the judge, "How does the defendant plead, Mr. Whistler?"

"Not guilty, your honour," snapped Mr. Whistler in a high, quarrelish voice.

At the trial seemingly directed at him, Dr. Baliles looked from one to another with amazement.

"Am I charged with something? With what am I charged?"

"Silence," said the judge, his upper lip twitching, his frown making him look ancient. "You, sir, will have ample opportunity to speak when you are placed on the witness stand. Until that time, let you keep silent. Uh, in regard to your charge, ah, hum, um. You will proceed with your case, Mr. Prosecutor."

Mr. Applegate rose, "I call for Dr. Albion Baliles to take the stand."

There was a pause. The clerk stepped forward.

"Do you swear to tell the truth, the whole truth, nothing but the - - - "

"Dr. Baliles, why are you in Waterford?"

"I didn't even know I was here."

"Ah, ah, then you claim insanity?"

"No no. I mean, I didn't know where I was," explained Dr. Baliles. "I was out driving and - "

"Ah ah, oh oh, hum hum," Mr. Applegate interrupted. "That will be all, Dr. Baliles. Judge Horsley, I have no further questions."

"Do you care to cross examine, Mr. Whistler?"

Mr. Whistler said nothing, sat in the comer looking at his papers and blowing quietly through his lips.

The judge continued, "Justice demands we allow the defendant every opportu nity to demonstrate the inadequacy of any proof against him: by the same token, it is imperative, the same opportunity be afforded the prosecution to fairly and accurately present its proofs against the defendant. With one accord, I hope, we can continue and so, come to a just verdict. You may call your next witness, Mr. Prosecutor."

"I would like to have Officer Oscar Shorb take the stand."

"Officer Shorb, take the stand," said the judge.

A tall, slim officer in a brown uniform walked to the witness box.

Then, the low mumble of the court clerk, "Do you swear to tell the truth, the whole truth, nothing but the —"

The light shone on the officer's receding forehead.

"Officer Shorb," said Mr. Applegate, "would you give the court a brief description of your duties and state your special instructions prior to the arrest of the defendant."

"My job, as police officer, is to keep order in the city of Waterford, apprehend any lawbreakers, put a cessation to any disturbance of the peace. I, as were other police officers, was told to expect, to look for, one Dr. Albion Baliles to arrive in the city in the immediate future; to arrest, to detain him."

"Am I correct in assuming you apprehended Dr. Baliles on the road. On the south side of the creek at the water's edge?"

"I did, sir. Just as I was told I would."

"And what was Dr. Baliles, when you first noticed, doing?"

"He was alookin' at the water."

"And do you see Dr. Baliles now present in this courtroom?" "That's him, sir, the defendant." Officer Shorb pointed.

"That is all," said the prosecutor. "Thank you, Officer. No more questions."

"Does the defense counsel care to cross examine?" stated the judge in a flat voice.

There was silence. There was no response.

"I object," called out the defendant.

"I beg your pardon?" said the judge, his voice showing surprise.

"First of all, I've not been in this city long enough to have transgressed against anyone. I have not been informed of what I am charged. I have not been given time to select and meet with an attorney. My defense counsel was not of my choice. He has been of no help at all. I would like to choose my own defense counsel."

The judge frowned. "Find most of the objections not pertinent to the case. Any further," the judge cleared his throat, "mention of them would be superfluous verbage. As to your legal counsel, however."

The judge cleared his throat. "May I ask, is it of your opinion that, as to the abilities of the attorneys, these are weighted more heavily in favor of the prosecution?"

"That's right," Dr. Baliles said loudly.

The judge looked thoughtful. "Um hum. May I see the defense counsel and the prosecutor in private consultation."

Mr. Whistler and Mr. Applegate walked to the front of the court. The judge chatted and chatted. The attorneys nodded and nodded. The judge, a grim smile, nodded. The attorneys went back to their places.

"Uh hum," the judge cleared his throat. "It is felt that the defendant has a right to a choice of attorneys. That, being there are only two attorneys in the city, Mr. Applegate, whom the defendant seems to favor, will now assume the duties of the defense attorney. Mr. Whistler will now become the prosecutor. There will be no need to put the defendant in gaol if the defense attorney will assume responsibility for his client. Court is recessed until tomorrow." He brought his gavel down with a bang.

The former prosecutor walked over, took off his spectacles. "Hello, I'm Arthur Applegate. Shall we adjourn to my place? The afternoon is young yet. There is always something to do at The Pillars, where I live. Then, my wife is always a good gamble for supper that's fit to eat. Then after supper, you can tell me about your case, perhaps, if you feel so inclined. Come."

Mr. Applegate led the way out of the room, through the dark hall, out into the warm afternoon sunlight; then, down to the path along the creek. Brushing back the foliage of green shrubs, here was a foot bridge of grey warped boards. Tromp tromp tromp went the feet on the bridge. They walked off to the left, onto the dirt covered stones of a street. Here along the cobblestone street were the stores the backs of which sat along the creek. Here, a square building, stone with bricks here and there in place of stones, tall shuttered windows above a sagging porch roof. Above the wide front door and two narrow windows to the left of the door, **R. J. Crowningshield Grocery.** Next to it stood a narrow building of whitewashed brick, the bricks on its upper right corner, broken and crumbled away. Visible but greyed letters across its brick front read **Evan Stelfox, We**

Buy We Sell. Then came a squat, dark blacksmith shop, a log front over a whitewashed stone foundation. Beyond the smithy stood a building of grey wood, its far wall tall so that its roof took a long drop to the low smithy which butted against its near wall. An old sign over its front door said **Farnsworth Hardware, Morgan Farnsworth, Proprietor.** With its cement barber pole, a small stone barbershop was next to the hardware; next, a tall brick building. Under an ornamental gable, a cement sign said **Sterling Apothecary.** Then, some trees were beyond a low stone wall; then, a little off the road, a mossy roofed brick building; then, off the road, a square stone building, a large chimney on its right side. Low shrubs covered the yard on either side of the mossy walk. There came some trees; then, there again, the ruined stone bridge.

From the bridge, the macadam road crossed and rose up the hill. Then the cobblestone road was a narrow dirt and gravel lane which ran through a sparsely wooded lot. To the right, beyond some trees, brush covered fields rose up into hillocks; then, to wooded hills. To the left, down through the trees, was an old mill.

"That's Stillpond Mill. It's pretty old," said Mr. Applegate. "The miller's family, the Fogwells, have been running it a long time."

The road came out into grass and brush covered hills sparsely covered with trees. The wooded creek bed bent to the left. To the right front, on the third hill over, stood a house of white brick, huge chimneys at either end. Beyond the house, tree covered hills. The men passed between two stone pillars.

The road went up, down a slope, passed around three white boulders, around and up among some slender trees, down a sunny slope, brambles and tall shrubs on either side of the road; then, through a tree filled valley, or gully, then up a weedy slope.

Dr. Baliles caught up with Mr. Applegate.

'Tell me, is the judge an old man? When he smiles, he looks young. When he frowns, really, he looks rather old."

"He is old," said Mr. Applegate, "but I don't know how old. My grandfather, in speaking of times passed, has spoken of the judge, Ourhouse Horsley, and I had gotten the impression that he was speaking of an age peer. Odd isn't it? That would make him very old indeed."

The road led them up through a narrow aisle between trunks of overhanging elms. It opened out in a field of tall weeds and summer flowers and to the front, at the top of a little rise, was the white brick house. Daises were in bloom. The fields here were awash with white. Dr. Baliles and Mr. Applegate walked through the daisies, through expanses blue with chicory, into a depression where milkweeds, yarrows and tall yellowed grasses grew. Two dogs barked. The men climbed a rise white with daisies, passed through a gate into a tree shaded front yard.

"The family would probably be in the drawing room," said Mr. Applegate as he walked toward a door on the left side of a long porch.

In the house, Dr. Baliles found himself in a high ceilinged room filled with massive, dark furniture: a table to the right rear, round with massive legs; a ceiling high secretary desk to the right of it; then, along the left wall, four wooden chairs with dark, carved backs and gold fabric seats. Behind the chairs, floor to ceiling bookcases stood. In the center of the right wall was a large fireplace. Off, to the far side of it; a stout, bald man sat reading a book. A huge, grey moustache graced his face and glasses on a black ribband clung to his nose.

"Uncle Howell, this is Dr. Baliles. Doctor, my uncle, Mr. Kilgour." Mr. Kilgour rose up, reached out his hand.

"How do you do, sir. I imagine Clive and Mr. Hardesty will be back before long. As far as I know, they were only going over to see the trial. Let's see, you're the defendant, Dr. Baliles?"

"Yes, that's correct, but I don't know yet what it's all about."

There were voices on the porch, two knocks. Mr. Applegate opened the door.

"Ah, Clive, Donald. Dr. Baliles, Mr. Prescott and Mr. Hardesty. Gentlemen, Dr. Baliles. And Doctor, I see we have two others coming. Gwen, Cole; Dr. Baliles. Doctor, Mr. and Mrs. Ogilvie."

"Ya. Gwen and Cole wanted to meet the defendant," said Mr. Prescott, his small moustache going up in a smile over his long chin, his high forehead wrinkling under wavy dark hair.

"We just couldn't resist the temptation," said Mr. Ogilvie, the sunlight glinting on his longish blond hair and large bright beard. "And I think Ni means to drop in too."

48

"Now we'd planned to do some hunting tonight and he could bring his dogs when he comes," said Mr. Applegate. "I'll just give him a ring. And Doctor, perhaps you'd like to freshen up a bit?"

"Yes, if I may." "Then this way."

Mr. Applegate led the way through the room to a back hall in which, in an alcove, was a marble top wash stand.

"Out that door is a path to the garden house. When you come back, pour yourself what water you need."

Mr. Applegate indicated a pitcher on the stand, then went through a door to his right.

Dr. Baliles walked out the door at the end of the hall, up a dirt path to an outhouse. He went in, raised the lid and sat. Out he came, down the path, past marigolds near the back hall door, and went in the door. He poured water into the bowl, washed, took a towel from a hook, dried his hands, and went into the library.

"Shall we get the chess back out?" said Mr. Hardesty, a slender, somewhat wrinkled, grayish gentleman. "Dr. Baliles, do you play?"

"Well, we have a game going here. You watch Prescott and me. Then you take on the winner."

Mr. Prescott was setting up a card table. Mr. and Mrs. Ogilvie were each dragging up a chair. Mr. Prescott got a chair, said "Get that chair there, Doctor."

Mr. Kilgour's grey vest puffed out and in. His gold watch fob shifted as he moved. He turned a page. The Ogilvies sat in chairs on the other side of the board, their backs to the dark fireless fireplace.

"Let's see. Bishop to king six." Mr. Hardesty was concentrating on his chess.

Mr. Applegate came back in. The wind blows in the big trees beyond the front porch. Mr. Prescott moved his queenside rook to queenside bishop one.

"Uncle Howell," Mr. Applegate asked his uncle, "Dr. Baliles' asking started me thinking about it. In age, how would you say Judge Horsley would compare to Grandfather? Older?"

"Than Owen? I hardly think so. That would make him pretty old wouldn't it? I'm not sure I know. You might ask old Billups when you see him. Likely Mr. Billups 'uld be able to tell you a thing like that." Mr. Kilgour raised his book.

The sinking sun shone red through the windows. The wind blew making speckled lead patterns dance in the red sunlight in the spots on the floor under the windows.

"One thing. Mr. Applegate, if I'm to be of any help to the defense counsel, I'm going to need to know with what I'm charged so I can deny the charge, affirm it or explain the circumstances, give the particulars. I asked that question in court today and the judge hemmed and hawed. I half expected to hear him say, 'I'm not certain I know the meaning of that term. One might, of course, be charged with electricity.' "

Mr. Applegate took off his spectacles, knocked them on the round black table beside him.

"I don't usually discuss business while I'm entertaining socially; or, in the places where I conduct my family and social affairs. Instead, I make an opportunity to take the business into my study. However, ah, in this case, there is so little to relate that I shall make an exception to my usual practice. All I know is, the judge called me, said he had wind of an Albion Baliles corning to town, that the man was dangerous, that the safest place for him would be in gaol, or court, until we found out more, more about it. The judge said he really didn't know a damn thing, wanted me to prosecute, set up a trial upon arrival. I said I would be an ass to prosecute without preparing a case, that I had never heard of it being done. He said time, stall, play it by ear, do the best you can. So, if you are, as you seem, an honest, upright professor type, I'll do my best to keep you from getting the business; but we've got to be sure, got to untangle this mess."

Dr. Baliles looked exasperated. He said, "The whole thing is insane. I was rendered speechless by the idiocy of it all. The judge must be off his rocker."

Mr. Applegate raised a finger, "The judge is a fine gentleman, honest and just. He has done a whole lot for me, a hell of a lot for the whole city of Waterford. He wouldn't have you in what is, in fact, a kangaroo court type situation unless he heard some danger bell and was afraid for the safety of the citizens of the town. Perhaps you know what he heard; but even if you told me, I wouldn't presume to say I was sure. For a start, have you any interest in this part of the country? Other than looking at the scenery? Then, you are a doctor. Have you specialized in fields of research which might be dangerous to us? And that could be lots of things: germ mutation, atomic energy development, livestock improvement, strip mining, modem city development. Tampering with our special type of Baldwin apples might annihilate an indescribable cider flavor, pungent beyond belief, found nowhere else in the world. That tree has been a target because it bears well only every other year, but that might be a blessing in disguise. But not to dwell on any one thing, one harmful thing, some doctor might eventually do, one might name others. Are you a carrier of something dangerous? Are you right now masking in some way?"

Mr. Applegate returned the dark rimmed spectacles to his eyes.

Dr. Baliles sat, looked puzzled. "There is just nothing. I don't know how I could possibly be dangerous. And how did he know I was coming? And who would care? I could just as soon have gone any, just any other direction when I left home."

"But for some reason, here you are."

There was a knock at the door. Mr. Applegate stepped over, admitted a slender young gentleman and three young ladies.

"Bridget, Becky, Elaine; this is Dr. Baliles. Doctor, Miss Avery, Miss Avery and Miss Avery." The girls giggled. "Doctor, this is Mr. Avery. Aneurin, Dr. Baliles."

Aneurin eagerly reached out a hand.

Mr. Applegate waved his arm, "You young folks drag up those chairs to suit yourselves. Would the company care to sample the wares of my wine cellar? Gwen, you'll have wine, won't you?"

"I'd love a glass of wine, thank you."

He turned to two small girls with pale, blond hair. "Elaine, Bridget? You girls are out of high school, aren't you?"

"Yes. Yes, thank you," said Elaine. Bridget smiled.

"Becky?" he asked a taller, big shouldered girl. A girl with soft, brownish blond hair hanging down to her shoulders.

"Oh, yes, thank you." "And you, Doctor?" "Yes please."

"Ni?"

"Um, please. Sounds good." "Uncle Howell?"

"You might bring me one, Arthur, please."

"And I know you others won't say no to a good glass of wine," said Mr. Applegate. He received affirmative nods, left the room.

Mr. Prescott wiped his fingers across his high, wrinkled forehead; picked up a knight, tapped it on the board a couple of times, moved it to his left. The men sat and looked at the pieces. The light in the room faded. The wind sighed.

Mr. Applegate returned with a tray filled with glasses of golden wine. "Our native scuppernong," he told the doctor. He passed wine to Gwen, to Becky, Bridget, Elaine, to Dr. Baliles, to Mr. Ogilvie. Mr. Hardesty picked up a knight, took the rook next to Mr. Prescott's king, took a glass of wine, held it and looked the board over.

"Since I am senior here, I propose the toast," said Mr. Kilgour. "Here's to things done: here's to great things, here's to kindly things, here's to things done just for the Hell of it."

The company drank.

The company sipped the wine. The breeze whistled around the comer of the house, rattled the loose, grey framed window. Dr. Baliles looked at the chess board, thought about it.

A high school age girl entered.

"Ah, Jill. This is Dr. Baliles, Jill. Doctor, my daughter, Jill." "Hi," said Jill. "Look at these."

She held up a wicker basket filled with bright marbles. "Elaine, Becky, look." She swung the basket over toward them. Mr. And Mrs. Ogilvie got up, went over to look. "See, Cole, I'm going to put them on the floor of the shrine."

She swung over toward Ni and Bridget who were coming over. Some of the marbles were quite small; some, large; some, large as hen's eggs. A few were as large as a man's fist. The company watched them shoot off rays of light as they sparkled, sparkled from transparent and translucent patterns which held a total spectrum of rainbow hues.

"Checkmate," said Mr. Hardesty rubbing his slender hands together; not smiling, but obviously pleased.

"Checkmate yourself," said a large but slender lady, slightly bent over, poking her face through the door at the back of the room.

"Dinner is served."

"That's my wife. Honey, this is Dr. Baliles. Doctor, my wife."

"How do you do, Dr. Baliles. You all be pleased to come in to dinner now."

The drawing room led to a back hall; small, dark, having in it a chest of dark wood. Then, the dining hall; a table, long under a white tablecloth, in its center. On the left, a long sideboard against a grey plaster wall. Light from the prism chandelier reflected off the shelf of blue china, off the glass ware over the sideboard. The company was directed, by Mrs. Applegate, to its places. At the end of the table, Mr. Applegate raised his hand, "In the name of the Father, the Son and the Holy Ghost." He crossed himself. "Bless, 0 Lord, these, thy gifts to us, and us to thy service. Amen." He picked up a bone handled carving set and carved a slice off the roast beef, passed a plate down, carved, passed another.

"Old Merrill will make an odd sort of prosecutor," said Mrs. Applegate.

"Merrill's a pretty sharp cookie. It's true he's a man of few words," said Mr. Applegate.

He passed a plate down the table.

The narrow, weathered face of Mr. Hardesty, to the right of Mr. Applegate, moved so the light caught in his light brown hair, leaned forward, "Doctor, not to belittle its accomplishments, but am I correct in saying, your clan hasn't yet discovered a cure for the common cold?"

Dr. Baliles looked over to his right. "I beg your pardon, I wasn't aware any of them were working on it."

"No, not your personal family of course," explained Mr. Hardesty, "But the whole genre of medical men."

Dr. Baliles nodded, sipped his coffee. "You're assuming I'm a medical doctor. I'm a PhD, an historian."

"You're a history professor?" asked Gwen Ogilvie, a small young woman, reddish blond hair done up on top of her head.

"No. At least I'm not presently teaching, but working for a current events magazine in Washington. I did teach though, before I came to Washington, at Dartmouth."

"I've suspected you were from New England," said Mrs. Ogilvie.

"No, from Rochester."

"Start the peas around, Clive, if you please, sir," said Mrs. Applegate.

Across the table, Mr. Prescott passed a brown and white dish toward his left.

To his right, Bridget took an ear of com off a blue platter, passed him the platter.

Mr. Applegate finished a row of com, put the ear down. "Ni, we're going to meet at Arch Holmead's. Stelfox, Manfred Sandidge and Charlie Binstead will meet us there, then we'll probably head out to the old Westfall place."

"Those bassets of Archibald's give you a musical evening," said Mr. Kilgour.

Becky was telling Elaine something at the other end of the table. The light flickered in the chandelier.

Mr. Applegate asked, "Won't you go with us, Doctor?"

"I think, if I may, I'll tum in early, thank you anyway."

"Yes of course. It's been a trying day for you," said Mr. Applegate.

"You can say that again," said the doctor.

The rest of the company were quietly eating. Way off somewhere, dogs were barking: several of them. Then, just one.

"You know, the church has gotten the Bingham Brothers to play for their picnic next Sunday," said Mr. Prescott.

"You going?" asked a man with a blond beard.

"Spect I might go, hear old Floyd fiddle some. He's one of the best. Then Algernon on his banjo. Algy's pretty good too."

"I hear they got Angus Cleghorn singing with them," said Mr. Ogilvie, the man with the beard.

"Blackie does?" Ni Avery asked. "He has the best voice of any man in our choir. He sure can sing church music."

"He sings at the shrine too," said Jill.

"Seems funny," said Mr. Hardesty, "sing at church; sing at the shrine too."

"God is everyplace," said Mr. Applegate. "Different facets, that's all. Your histories would seem to affirm that, wouldn't they, Doctor? Same God, different ways to worship the same God?"

"Quite true. There is evidence of that."

Becky said, "Father Atwater said, if it weren't for Christmas, we might all be Hindus."

"Supposing Christ to have been born on Christmas, that is," said Mr. Ogilvie.

Mrs. Applegate was saying something in a low voice to someone on her left, then to Becky.

"You going out with us this evening, Uncle Howell?" Mr. Applegate asked. He ate a fork full of Yorkshire pudding.

"No, not tonight, Arthur. I get too used to going to bed at regular hours."

The light glinted off the shiny silverware as the company ate.

"More roast, Yorkshire pudding, Doctor?" asked Mr. Applegate.

"No, I thank you. I've enjoyed it though. Better Yorkshire pudding I don't recall having eaten."

"More of this for you others? Gwen? Becky? Bridget? Elaine? Any of you men? Uncle Howell, how about you?" The company finished eating.

"Gwen, you may help me clear up, if you like,"·said Mrs. Applegate. The ladies rose. Gwen came up, got Mr. Applegate's, Dr. Baliles' plate, carried them away. Across the room, the light from the chandelier made bright spots on the greyed plaster wall. Gwen and Mrs. Applegate each brought in a pie. Gwen sat down. Mrs. Applegate sliced a pie, passed a section down. Jill handed Dr. Baliles the pot of coffee.

"You know, little Doug Musselwhite fell out of a swing and broke his arm," said Gwen.

"I know," said Mrs. Applegate, "I'll make some candy, take it to him tomorrow."

"You sure make the best cherry pie in the world," said Mr. Prescott. "I'll say," said Mr. Avery.

"Sure is."

Mrs. Applegate finished her coffee.

"Come, let us get on our way," said Mr. Applegate, getting up.

The company arose. Mr. Applegate, Mr. Avery, Mr. Prescott, Mr. Ogilvie and Mr. Hardesty started toward the door at the far end of the room.

"See you at breakfast, Doctor," said Mr. Applegate. "Goodnight," said Mr. Hardesty.

"It was my pleasure, Doctor," said Mr. Prescott near the door, shaking hands.

Mr. Avery shook hands, Mr. Ogilvie waved and went out.

"Now any time you like, Doctor, I can show you your room," said Mrs. Applegate, "Or, after we girls clean up, we can help Uncle Howell entertain you."

"Thank you, if it weren't for tomorrow's trial, I'd stay up. As it is, I'm about ready to take a look at that room now."

"This way then." Mrs. Applegate led the way out the door; into the kitchen, smoky dark walls; around a black iron range; up a dark, curving back stairs. A door at the top led to a small room; the plaster, greyed orangey in colour. A clear glass coal oil lamp sat on a square dark wood table; the table, the other side of a narrow bed with a pale carved headboard; the headboard, against the right wall. Smoke rose up the tall, glass chimney in a thin stream. On the wall, beyond the

56

foot of the bed, a small window looked out to the back yard.

"The outhouse is out there, back of the flower beds, case you're wantin' it."

"Thank you," said the doctor.

Mrs. Applegate went out.

To the right of the door stood a marble top wash stand. And on it, a porcelain bowl and pitcher. Across from the door, beyond the bed, a dark wardrobe looked over the room, its high top curved up in a circular design. To its left, a wooden Windsor style chair and that, between the wardrobe and a square bureau of pale wood. A mirror on a small, dark single drawer cabinet and that on the bureau, reflected the yellow light from the lamp. Dr. Baliles walked around the foot of the bed, took off his pants, put them on the chair, took off his coat, his shirt, got into bed, lay and listened to the wind over the house and in the trees out back. On the bureau, a red orange pottery dog looked fierce in the flickering light. The flickery light reflected off the greenish grey vase; the vase, on the fire side of the dog; flickered on the walls making spidery cracks seem to wiggle. Over the door, a blank faced angel of pale pottery reached out a wing toward each end of the bed; its face, as blank as an egg. The wind whistled and sighed. The shadow of a web wavered on the angel's face almost giving it features; sad, melancholy features, dark across the eyes. The wind sighed. The doctor shut his eyes.

There was a tap at the door.

"Yes?" said the doctor, opening his eyes. "It's Jill. I come in?"

"Yes of course."

The door opened. Jill stood there in a white, a transparent, nightgown; a worn, brown satchel in her hand. "Officer Shorb brought it. I thought you might be wantin' it before breakfast." She set it down.

"Thanks. Indeed I'd feel lost without it."

Jill stood, a draft billowing out her nightgown slightly, then letting it drop. "You're not married," said Jill.

"No, but I'm engaged." "I thought not," she said.

The wind blew outside. Jill's nightgown billowed out behind her — hung still. The wind sighed, sighed outside. Jill waved, stepped out and shut the door. The wind blew loudly in a whistling sigh. Something somewhere swayed back and forth. Dr. Baliles turned down the wick. The light got bluish — went out.

It was dark. Dr. Baliles reached out his left arm, felt nothing; reached behind him, ran his hand over the headboard. He curled up in the bed and lay still. There was silence. Somewhere the floorboards creaked. All was still. Dr. Baliles lay in the still silence.

A rooster crowed - another rooster. The room was light, the walls bright with yellow light. Outside the little window, the clouds were salmon pink and bright gold. "Dr. Baliles, are you up? We'll serve breakfast shortly," Mrs. Applegate called up the stairs.

Dr. Baliles got up. "Yes, thank you," he called down.

Dr. Baliles put on his pants, his shoes, as the room got brighter; then, out onto the dark stairs, down past the kitchen table, out the screen door, into the fresh, cool air. He walked on the path through the brown dirt yard - between two beds bright with red cannas, to a whitewashed outhouse. It was warm and dark inside. Then, back to the house, through the kitchen, up the curving stairs. He hunted in his leather bag, went to the marble top, poured water on his toothbrush. The water on his toothbrush was cool. He washed in the cool water.

"Ah, Dr. Baliles, breakfast," called Mrs. Applegate.

Dr. Baliles went down, through the kitchen, to the dining hall. At the table, Mr. Applegate, Jill, Mr. Kilgour and Mr. and Mrs. Ogilvie were taking their places. Golden butter and a pot of honey stood at each end of the table. Mrs. Applegate brought in steaming corncakes on a platter. She put cakes on Gwen's plate, on Mr. Ogilvie's.

"We go to the shrine today," said Jill. "You can come with us if you want, Dr. Baliles."

"That's quite an honour they confer on you, Doctor," said Mr. Applegate.

"They've never let Cole or Ni go with them when they were doing something at the shrine."

"But I can't feel picked on," said Mr. Ogilvie. "After all, even Jack

Mooney, whom most of the girls find glamorous, isn't invited; nor, are Frank or Ralph Musselwhite. And they haven't invited Neil Hitchcock."

"Not Neil? I thought he was pretty special," said Mr. Applegate. "He is," said Jill. "But not that special."

"The bulls take precedence over Neil," said Mr. Kilgour. "The bulls come first," said Jill. She ate some corncake.

"Thank you, I'd love to go. If it's in the morning, of course."

Jill put down her fork. "It's just most men aren't the shrine type. Some, like Father Atwater, go another route. At a dance, at a picnic, Neil is special. Gwen, we'd like to have you come. Cole, you still can't come. Some other time, maybe. Mind, no promise. But we could never have those others."

"Alright, alright." Cole laughed. "I'll find some other joy."

The company ate. Mrs. Applegate took the platter, went to the kitchen.

Dr. Baliles looked up at Mr. Applegate. "How'd the hunting go? Did you get a coon?"

"Oh, the dogs treed a coon, but we didn't take any guns. Probably the same old coon we'd treed last time. We go just to give the dogs a run. And to hear some of Stelfox's lies."

"And to tell some yourself," said Mr. Kilgour.

"Of course. Yes, quite so," said Mr. Applegate.

"Is taking pictures allowed?" Gwen asked.

Jill looked thoughtful. "Some. You can bring your camera. Be sure to ask before you shoot. Some things should be graphically recorded, like for historic reasons. You should appreciate that, Doctor."

"I wasn't aware, we were dealing with a thing of special historic interest. I mean, more than the town itself is. The Still Pond Mill, for instance, interests me. I'm interested in the origin of its name, for one thing," said the doctor.

"I don't know that it's ever occurred to any of us to enquire," said Mr. Applegate.

"No, I myself have asked," said Mr. Kilgour, "but I've never been able to discover what that origin might have been."

Mrs. Applegate entered, put comcakes on one plate, on another. Bright sunlight streamed in the window, the light through the old glass making wavery patterns on the white tablecloth. It glinted in bright spots on the glassware, on the silverware, on the brown pepper mill.

"But as an historian, Doctor," Mr. Kilgour continued, "you should take interest in our local shrine. To compare the antiquity of that with that of the mill, you do the shrine injustice. You might be thinking, because of a recent trend toward one world consciousness; people, especially young people, having become interested in religions out of their heritage; are following a fad of setting up places which imitate sacred places of distant lands or times and that this would be one of those. And certainly many new shrines have sprung up for the practicing of religions which, for the people at those new shrines, would be foreign, strange, exotic and new. But our shrine is not a shrine newly set up. Until recently, we called it the Cave of the Bulls and most people never thought of it in connection with religion. The only religion that they here knew about was that put forth by our local parish. Then, the bulls themselves were covered over by ancient boxwood. Much of this has died out, been removed. With the thinking on religion changed, our young people have revived an interest in the cave. As to antiquity, in speaking of the mill, in speaking of the shrine, it is not to use the word antiquity in the same way. The mill might be three hundred years old. The shrine was old when the Yougohomeny tribe, now extinct, lived in these parts. And they knew as little about it as we do: less than I, because they called it the Cave of the Buffalos; but these bovine obviously aren't buffalo. I sent pictures of them to Clarence Still in Washington. He sent word that they are representations of a breed of cattle extinct for nearly a thousand years, wondered where the pictures were taken. I told him Greece, for obvious reasons. As to their age, he might be mistaken, but we know they must be ancient. And I got a letter from antiquarian Cecil Osgood Zogg, still under the impression, mind you, that I had obtained the photographs from Greece. He thanked me for sending them, saying he was interested in them because of their similarity to representations of a beast associated with Beli, with Baal, with Pellinore and with Balin of the Isle. And I got a letter from Dr. Hugo

Howard Ocasey, sort of an antiquarian, not at all under an illusion that the pictures came from Greece. In keeping with his studies, he had anticipated such relics in this area — told me he was coming to see me. He got someone, a friend perhaps, to rent a car for him, put on a disguise, drove to Waterford."

"And shot the man who rented him the car," the doctor suggested.

"You're being facetious. And Waterford's not a good town to be facetious in. He came, said he could appreciate my desire for secrecy, made a few recommendations to do with further secrecy, more security, looked at the relics himself and I gave him pictures. Now you might think it rather selfish of me to keep to myself what one might think should be declared a national treasure; but as soon as something becomes a national treasure, it takes on an air of artificiality. And what would happen to the city of Waterford should multitudes of John Jones and Joe Blows beat a path to here? The city, which is, as you say, histori cally interesting, would either be demolished or put in a goldfish bowl. You would no longer see a functioning bit of the past, but someone else's idea of what antiquity should be like. You know the trip: Revolution age houses located, the dirt swept away, niceties added, until a poor working man's house looks like the house of a lord and that, the rare lord with a household of servants who work with mechanical efficiency. Some forget, antiquities in their day were the common place, used and misused, fine things neglected, left kicking around unpolished and uncleaned. So, keeping this in mind, you mightn't be surprised to find a visiting historian, even one with a special interest in current events, made somewhat unwelcome by those of us aware of the dangers. History, I'm led to believe, is not just dates, battles and politics; but is concerned with all aspects of living: with customs, arts, religious trends and such. And shrines, as you understand, are current. The judge might hope to make you so unwelcome that you would never come back. When you mentioned the mill, I was tempted to offer, instead of that to the shrine, a walk to the mill, to try to persuade you to go that route. And you and I would have looked for evidences of still ponds and looked at other interesting and informative things until time for your case to be tried. But should you have declined the offer, you would have been under no obligation to us not to make yourself famous by research into what must prove newsworthy. Common sense tells us we can't put you in gaol and throw away the key. I thought it best to explain our situation, ask your understanding cooperation. How did the judge know you were coming? Maybe you stopped for gas, used a credit card along the way. You people in Washington use them for everything, I'm told."

"I don't recall that I did," the doctor said.

"But I wasn't aware of any of this," said Mr. Applegate.

"It's best," said Mr. Kilgour. "You all know. And, too, the urgency for secrecy. And Jill, Honey, I don't know how seriously you girls take your dancing and singing at that spot, but keep in mind, please, those heads may once have been worshipped as gods. I should advise they be treated with respect and with some caution."

"We do, Uncle Howell. Some day you shall come with us and see."

"Well, I'll have a word with the judge," said Mr. Applegate. "Perhaps this mess can be straightened out, Dr. Baliles be more generally made welcome."

"I'd be much obliged," said Dr. Baliles.

The company got up. There was a knock on the door. Mr. Applegate walked out of the room. He came back in and with him, an old gentleman dressed in coarse green tweed, his face hidden behind a white mustache and short, full white beard.

"Dr. Baliles, this is Mr. Humphrey Billup; Mr. Billup, Dr. Albion Baliles," said Mr. Applegate.

"Will you have a cup of coffee, Mr. Billup?" Mrs. Applegate asked.

"No, I thank you just the same. Can't stay. I only wanted to meet Dr. Baliles, wish him luck. The only advice, and you probably know it, let them do the talking, say little as possible."

"Thank you, Mr. Billup," said Dr. Baliles.

"Well, I'll bid you good day." He shook hands with the doctor.

The company walked with Mr. Billup into the next room; past, on their left, a stairway, the shiny balustrade making a decorative effect against the wall. They walked across the dark floor, between a large brick fireplace, on the left, and, on the right; a chair, a sofa, two chairs upholstered in rose; walked to a door. Mr. Billup went out.

The light came from two windows to the left of the door. It shone on the odd shaped, shiny wood carvings on the brown mantle. Mr. Billup was seen through the window, trudging down the road.

Mr. and Mrs. Applegate, then the company, walked through a door to the right of the fireplace, into a small room.

"This is the family parlour," said Mrs. Applegate. "A place where we can relax, be ourselves, as you see by the homemade art on the walls. Jill's," she waved at the handsome abstracts. Narrow, nearly four feet tall, one to either side of a dark captain's chest; then, at the rear wall, over an upright piano. "And by my needlework covering these old wooden chairs, more comfortable than they look: by Arthur's, he calls them antiques, worn out billows, old mismatched shovel and tongs; and that lemon of a spinning wheel that's never worked right." She pointed to where it stood against the wall near the billows; "And by my dime store vase, Jill's china dog on the mantle and, and by that thing." She pointed to the rear comer, left of the piano.

"She means my totem pole, of course," said Mr. Kilgour.

Mrs. Applegate sat in a shiny wood rocking chair in front of the fireplace, put her arms on the wooden arms and rocked. Mr. and Mrs. Ogilvie crossed in front of the fireplace, sat in chairs on that side. Mr. Kilgour sat in a low, round backed chair to the right of Mrs. Applegate. Mr. Applegate took a chair to the right of that. Jill crossed the room, sat on cushions on the captain's chest. Dr. Baliles walked to the tall bookcase which stood, against the right wall, between two windows. He stood and looked at the books: children's books, cookbooks, books on nature. He turned, saw Jill motion him over, went over and sat beside her.

"Indeed, I think this, a handsome room," said Dr. Baliles.

Mr. Applegate put his feet up on the cobbler's bench in front of his chair.

"I want to know lots of things," said Jill. "What you enjoy, what you did and what books you read when you were little."

"Such pleasures would take years to tell," said the doctor.

"This room has seen its good times," said Mr. Ogilvie.

Mrs. Applegate said, "Those magazines aren't re.al new, but

perhaps there are some you'd like to take to your room." She nodded toward the magazine rack, the opposite side of the fireplace from the billows, stuffed overflowing with magazines. "We'd like you to stay a while in Waterford, if you'd so honour us." She stood up. "Let me fill the coffee cups."

"We should be going, Mother," said Jill. She got up.

"But don't let that stop you from filling the cups," said Mr. Applegate.

"Come, Gwen," said Jill. She and Dr. Baliles left the room, crossed a dark floor, went out a door into a narrow hall; past, to the right, a door with a brass name plate, a tall hat tree. Jill stopped by the front door, picked up her marbles off an umbrella stand, went out into bright sunshine. The door banged. Mr. and Mrs. Ogilvie came out. Jill and Dr. Baliles with the Ogilvies, walked out under dark shadows of trees, out to the road.

"Here, you carry these," Jill gave the doctor the basket. "Gwendolyn is sort of new here too. She's a Carolinian."

"Charleston's loss is our gain," said Mr. Ogilvie. "We met at William and Mary. Been married about six months. Goodbye for now."

"So long," said Dr. Baliles.

Gwen and Cole went down the road.

Dr. Baliles and Jill walked into a round, sloping field of daisies. Jill stopped, picked the flowers.

"Now this is the way to make a daisy chain." She wove daisies in and out until she had a necklace.

"Ah, you've made yourself a necklace," said the doctor.

"No, made you a necklace." She held it out and over it went. She took an arm and they walked arm in arm down the slope, into a weedy bottom, across a dirt lane, up a finger of land rising to the right, covered with scrubby woods. Walking along the top, they passed a projection going down to the right, passed another. On the third projec tion down, they took a path. The woods got denser. They walked through the dense green, down to a damp valley of flowers. Across the valley was the bending creek.

They crossed the valley to where the creek entered the woods. To their right, the land rose up. They came to cliffs of grey and white rock. The cliffs bent right, formed a little dell. Shrubs and trees grew dense in front of the cliffs, were thick on the other side of the creek where the ground rose up. Moss and fems covered the floor of the dell. To the right, in front of the cliffs, stood a series of flat boulders: seven pale boulders like huge irregular tombstones; the tallest, over ten feet in height. To the rear, right and left of the stones, were tall, scraggly boxwoods. In front of the rear and largest stone, a marble pedestal held a crystal globe. Behind the largest stone, in the rocky cliff, was the dark mouth of a cave. On either side of that mouth, jutting out from the face of the cliff, staring out over the top of the standing stones, just out of reach, if one stood under them, were two giant bull's heads of snow white, ornately carved marble, white as snow in the morning sun. The heads were three to four times the size of the heads of any living bulls. Their delicate lines, in curves and curls, shimmered in the brightness and prism like, shattered rays of light.

A tall girl came out of the trees beyond the cave. Her pale hair picked up the light, was bright in the sunshine.

"That's Charlotte Talbot," said Jill. Charlotte came up. "Charlotte, this is Dr. Baliles."

Charlotte smiled at Dr. Baliles, said, "I guess I was the first here." She waved.

Dr. Baliles looked around. Two girls were coming into the dell.

"There are Polly Carmody and Jane Stelfox." The girls came up, slender girls: one brown haired, one, with darker hair. "Polly, Jane, this is Dr. Baliles. Come, let us gather flowers to put on the bulls."

They all walked out of the dell, into the sunny field of flowers. Here, coming toward them across the field, were Becky, Bridget and Elaine Avery and another girl was with them. Elaine came up, took the doctors hand, said, "You chickened out on our party last night."

"I'll make the next one." Dr. Baliles smiled. "I wanted to think some about the trial."

"Did you?"

"I went to sleep."

"Maybe I should have sat on your chest and kept you awake," said Jill. The other girls laughed.

"Doctor," said Elaine, "Our friend here is Elizabeth Janney. We call her Libby.

She's like a pretty little younger sister. Libby, come give the nice doctor a hug." Libby came up, hugged and kissed the doctor.

"Oh Doctor, you're beautiful. You don't stick things in people I hope? But even if you do, I'm sure it won't hurt."

"No, Libby, he's a professor," said Jill. "Come let's pick flowers for the bulls. It's they are priority."

"We should think of them now," said Polly. "Honour them with thoughts as pure as snow."

She began picking flowers. The others picked flowers. A girl approached from the dell.

"There's Rhonda Tremayne." Jill straightened up. "Rhonda, this is Dr. Baliles."

"Hi," said Rhonda. She started picking flowers as she came toward the others. Two red haired girls entered the field of flowers. They walked toward the others, smiles and dimples on their freckled faces.

"There are Sally Ann and Alice," said Libby.

"Sally Ann, how is Doug? Doctor, you heard us talking about Doug Musselwhite. These are his sisters."

He's just fine. Except the cast, you'd never know he'd broken anything. I see we have Dr. Baliles with us. Hi, Doctor. I'm Sally Ann."

"And I, Alice."

"Hi, Sally Ann, Alice."

The red haired girls joined the others in picking flowers. Great bunches of flowers were gathered.

Jill said, "Let's sit in a circle and make chains."

Armfuls of flowers were gathered up and the girls, with the doctor, formed a circle, sat down and Dr. Baliles with them. They

66

started weaving two thick chains; mostly, with the white and gold of daisies with some pink flowers, some blue chicory flowers. A girl was coming across the field from the direction of the bridge: a trim, big shouldered well developed girl; perhaps college age. She walked up. Jill introduced her.

"Doctor, this is Constance Cooley. Connie, please meet Dr. Baliles."

"Hi," said the doctor.

"Hello." Connie sat in the circle to the right of Libby, Sally Ann and Alice; began helping Alice with the flowers. She brushed her long brown hair away from her face.

Dr. Baliles looked from the trim, robust Musselwhite sisters to the slender but muscular Connie, to the flowing figure of Rhonda, then at other girls even more slender. "A god couldn't want for a more beautiful priesthood."

"Thank you, Doctor. You flatter us," said Becky.

A girl was coming up from the river, from near the cliffs. Jill looked up. "There is Minerva Mooney. She's been away at college. Hi, Minnie."

Minnie came up in a quick walk; a tall girl with long, dark hair and longish, dark silky hair on her slender forearms.

"Minnie, this is Dr. Baliles." "Hi," said Minnie.

"Hi, girls."

She sat by Rhonda, a girl with dark, auburn hair, and helped weave the flowers.

The chains were getting long.

Jill said, "Let's take our chains and, Doctor, my basket into the cave."

She got up, Dr. Baliles with her, the others following. They walked through the field of flowers, along the creek to the dell, then up to the stones which were standing five feet and taller, then past the tallest stone, the stone behind the crystal globe, and as they passed, their moving reflections, distorted, floated across the globe. Then, into the dusk, the company filed into the cave. Jill lit white candles which stood on a stone brilliantly coloured in ornate arabesques so that the stone seemed an ideal, nature made altar. Along each wall, bright colours wiggled and flowed into the shapes of stalactites and stalagmites, blossomed into shapes like deep sea, underwater flowers. Shapes in bright crystals blazed; piles of crystals covered the floor, glistening in every colour. Jill walked ahead into a roundish room lower down than the first. She lit a candle, lit another candle, a third, a fourth, a fifth, a sixth, a seventh, an eighth, a ninth. The tall white candles stood along the left wall. This room, too, was bright with the colours in the twisty rocks.

"Now," said Jill, "We will change into our robes. That means you too, Doctor.

Take off your clothes."

The girls began taking off their clothes. Dr. Baliles took off his shirt, his pants.

"Where is my robe? " he asked.

"We will fit you with one," said Jill.

Already naked, Elaine stood next to the doctor, her pale skin glowing in the light from the tall, white candles.

"Come hurry along, Doctor. You aren't ready yet with underpants on, you know," she said.

Dr. Baliles took off his underpants. The girls, all naked, were looking through the stack of white gowns. Minnie was bringing over a white robe, her nakedness emphasizing, accentuating, the jet darkness of her hair. She walked up in front of the doctor, put the shiny white robe around his shoulders. Jill came up, her white gown hung over her arm. She checked the fit of the doctor's robe.

"That looks right," she said.

She put her white gown over her head, the gauze like material shimmering in the soft light from the candles.

Minnie walked back to where the other girls were putting on gowns of that sheer white cloth. Jill bent down, picked up the marbles from beside the doctor's pants. "Come," she said. She and the other girls walked toward the forward chamber, stepped up into it. Jill walked to the altar, stopped in front of it, her basket she raised high over her head. The other girls formed a semicircle behind her, sang, "O holy light, 0 Lord of the White Shafts of the Morning, thank you." She knelt, touched the basket to her heart; stood, offered it to the North, East, South, West; scattered the bright marbles on the floor about the altar. The marbles rolled and mingled with the bright rock crystals which made up the floor. Jill walked toward the cave entrance. The others followed; out, into the dell, joined hands, moved around in a dance.

"Good Doctor, please move out in the center more so we can get around you more easily," said Jill.   ·

Around they danced in a circle, weaving in and out; half going one way; half the other. As they danced, they sang, "I asked him then to truly tell me, how many strawberries grow in the salt sea. He answered me then as true as he could, as many's red herrings that swim in the wood. In Notaman Town my soul looked down. Not a soul looked up, not a soul looked down to show me the way to fair Notaman Town. The beggar rich and the bishop poor kept riding behind, kept walking before, kept riding behind, kept walking before, kept riding behind, kept walking before, to show me the way to Notaman Town. A stark naked drummer then did come, his hands in his pockets and beating his drum, his hands in his pockets and beating his drum; his hands in his pockets, he whistled a song. I ride a white horse which is a grey mare, grey mane and grey tail, grey stripes -" The dancing stopped. Gwen was coming up from the river.

She was dressed in green with her red gold hair combed out long.

"Gwen, you will want one with us in a circle around the doctor, like we're being blessed; then, do bless us too," said Jill.

Gwen held up her camera and took a picture.

"Now Gwen, we're going to make a flower wreath around Dr. Baliles' neck. You can help us," said Jill.

The girls walked down to the entrance of the dell, by the creek, out into the field of flowers, started picking; the green dress, bright in the bright sunshine; the white gowns, whisps around slender naked bodies. The doctor stood at the entrance to the dell and watched. The girls brought the flowers back to the dell, sat in a circle in the center of the dell, wove flowers into chains, wove the chains together. The doctor stood beside them. Jill and Polly stood up, brought the garland to the doctor, hung it on his neck.

"Catch this, Gwen," said Jill.

Gwen took the picture.

"Now the wreaths for the bulls," said Jill. "Libby, Alice, get the wreaths."

Libby and the red haired Alice stood up, went into the cave; came back, each with a wreath.

"Let me put it on. I need somebody to hold me." Libby held her wreath in front of her.

Jill took the wreath of the doctor. "Put Libby on your shoulders, Doctor, please."

The doctor bent over. Libby, pulled up her gown and sat on the doctor's neck, wriggled around to get comfortable. She was warm and damp. The doctor stood up, walked to the left hand bull. Libby looked up.

'I'm going to have to stand on your shoulders."

She put her feet on the doctor's shoulders, stood up. Dr. Baliles put his hands up to steady her. Jill stood by, watching.

"Not outside, Doctor. You'll tear her gown. Reach under her gown and hold her legs. And watch what you're doing. That's it. Libby, you're still too short."

Libby sat back down on the doctor's shoulders, slid off. "Here, let me," said Becky.

"Or else me," said Minnie.

"Becky, I think Minnie's a little taller," said Jill.

Minnie came up, pushed the doctor down, sat on his neck. The doctor stood up and Minnie stood on his shoulders. The doctor put up his hands to steady her.

"Now hand me that, Libby." She put the garland over the bull, sat back down, her gown going over the doctor's head, down nearly to his waist.

"OK, the other." Minnie reached for the other wreath. "How's that for a picture," said Jill. "Don't shoot it though."

The brown haired Polly handed Minnie the other garland. The doctor walked around to the other bull. Minnie stood up, dropped the garland over the head, sat back down, pulled up her gown and slid off to the ground.

"Now," said Jill, "Catch all of us under the bulls. Doctor, stand in front by the globe. Here, put on your wreath."

Gwen backed off, took the picture. "Now a picture of the doctor and a bull."

"Could you climb to that ledge of rock by the head?" Gwen asked.

"No, I don't think so. But I could walk around, drop down, step over to it."

He walked down along the cliff toward the gap. The girls waited. He climbed over a low cliff, walked up to the cave, climbed down over a head. The girls stood watching. He dropped. "Damn." The marble smashed. It was eggshell thin. Rotten bone, rotten brains, up to the hips in black, putrid mush; the splintered, caved in skull smelling of death. Plop. On the ground with the doctor; a mass of black blood; smashed rotten bone, rotten flesh, broken teeth, a torn piece of tongue. Above the doctor, a black pit, a black cavity in putrid flesh, a stinking darkness, the stench filling the air. Across the way, the other bull's head cracked open, dripped black fluid, black flesh oozing out of the split. The girls gasped, horror stricken, stared at the head smashed faceless, a jagged mass of rotten flesh, stared at the white robe covered with vile black. Libby, Rhonda, Charlotte, Elaine sank to the ground. The right head split wider, dripped blood. The girls cried.

"Take off that disgraced robe," said Jill. She sunk to the ground beside the ruined flesh.

Minnie, standing behind her, wiped tears away with her fists. Bridget sat, looked up at the cliff, cried. Connie, Polly, Alice, Sally Ann and Becky pulled the robe off the doctor. Minnie went over, pulled his head down. Jane slapped his rear. Connie, Polly, slapped, slapped, slapped. They slapped it pink. Saily Ann rolled the doctor over. Alice slapped his stomach.

"I'm going to water his shrubbery," said Libby.

She straddled the doctor, pulled up her gown, bent her knees, pissed on his stomach. Minnie picked up the doctor's knees. Jane rubbed mud on his rear.

"I'm going to piss in his ear," said Connie, squatting over the doctor's head. "Turn your head, idiot."

"No, stop," said Jill. "That's not allowed."

"Why?" Connie asked.

"Why? Well do it and find out why."

Connie stood up.

"Idiot, if you'd turned your head, I'd have pissed already. Take that."

"aah."

"Stop it. Stop kicking him because I said something. You aught to be glad he didn't turn his head. You aught to be God damn glad."

Connie started crying. "We're supposed to be holy and look at us. And you swearing like that."

Jill fell to the ground and cried. The other girls stood and cried. The doctor asked, "May I get dressed?"

"Stay where you are," said Jill.

Connie walked over to a clump of fems, pulled up her gown, squatted, pissed.

Jill looked up at the doctor, "Kneel under that head and pray for pardon."

"I will not. I won't be told when to pray."

"No, I can't command prayer." Jill put her hands to her mouth and cried.

Gwen went and sat by the doctor. "I feel rotten about this," she said. "They should have taken their anger out on me."

Jill said, "No, Gwen, you're not to blame. Those heads were marble and solid in the cliff or I would have said something. I stood by and let him. But I thought he was pure." Tears ran from her eyes "And he wouldn't even warn us."

"Well as far as I know, I am pure. I'm one of the few people my age who have never experienced sex. And I have the normal appetites."

"Then you're blasphemous. Or, false hearted," said Jill. She melted into the ground, her eyes flooding with tears.

Gwen asked, "Why have you waited so long? Sex I mean?"

"Been engaged a long time. Wanted to start fresh with marriage."

"Why engaged so long?" Gwen wanted to know.

"Because I began to suspect the ying yang wouldn't perfectly mesh.

Jill said, "I wouldn't have sat still waiting for the ying tang to mesh."

"Demanded marriage? You might have pulled it off," said the doctor.

"No, I wouldn't have pulled it off. I would have waited to be told I was your perfect, eternal love. You, waiting, would have crushed me, thrown me to the winds. Maybe I broke the heads. Today should have been so perfect: A real, real special holy day; a white knight, I thought, come to honour it, to love us. I knew you had psychic powers, could feel them. And the judge jumping around, like when Dr. O'Casey came. But you didn't love enough. Now everything is just smashed to pieces; the life is crushed out of me. There is nothing left. And the poor heads bleeding their life out." Jill lay on the ground and cried and cried.

"Jill, fight back. You're the priestess, hold things together," said the doctor.

"No, that's smashed too, dripping out with the blood. I'm nothing. I broke it." She bit her fist and cried. The other girls cried.

"Come," said Gwen, "I'll wash you off in the creek." She and the doctor went down to the creek. Gwen slipped out of her green dress, her panties. "My husband and I allow each other this much freedom." She knelt by the water, pulled the doctor down in, washed off rotten blood. She lay by the water, pulled up her knees, splashed water between the doctor's legs.

"This is close to what they call the sixty nine position," she ran her fingers gently, firmly. "Sure it's alright?" She raised her leg. "You have gentle hands. Ah. Ah." She went limp. "Um. There we hit just about together. Um, beautiful." She drew up her knees more, and shut her eyes. She turned around, snuggled up close. "Now, if any should ask, you can say you are sort of," Gwen giggled, "experienced by half. Our marriage is best when, on rare and chosen occasions, my husband and I have shared out most tender affections with persons outside our home. We return home deepened, enriched. Some years ago, I might not have understood this. Perhaps I learned it at college. Why didn't you take her in your arms, tell her she was your perfect, eternal love?"

"Because I wasn't sure."

"I was."

Gwen's embrace was warm and tight.

"In a minute I'll be experienced by more than half," said the doctor.

"No, no, I think you should wait. It will mean a lot to Jill if you do."

"Yes, of course it will. I was sure you'd say that. And I'm glad."

"There's a certain atmosphere between you and Jill. It is very pure. But it will take some doing to bring her old sparkle back. She's crushed. Lost not only her princess status, but I think something really has died. Albion?"

"I know. It's this mystic quality. This unexplainable mystery's had me buffaloed. There's a chance, I thought, that sexuality was an intrusion on pure spirituality, but surely this wasn't the first occasion the two were combined. I'm not blasphe mous, profane. If I was unworthy, it was not to my knowing. We haven't yet explained the mystery and I let myself be completely controlled by an out of control bunch of girls who, priestesses though they may be, are really pretty young. I'm the one that should be mature. Things have gotten way out of proportion. It's time I took the bull by the horns, so to speak: became assertive."

"Albion, I agree. Though, without so speaking. I mean, the expression is, shall we say, inopportune. No, I don't think, sexy though you are; and a touch, blasphemous, too; that you caused our misfortunes. The great mystics are often somewhat blasphemous. And a bull would understand an erection. If you hadn't killed the

74

bulls, I think someone else would have. Jill suggests her falling in love caused their death. Maybe it was the other way around."

"I feel really bad that I killed the bulls, even by accident. That's the hard part, they felt alive. When people die, it doesn't help to say they were old, had to die. Death is tragic. The only thing that helps me, when those I love die, is to think of death as a thing which I will share with them, though in my own time. I am still sad, though, for those I have loved, and for those I would have loved, who have died, even though they might have died centuries ago. So we cry when things die."

"I cried for the bulls too. We should go up."

She put her lips hard against the doctor's mouth, stood up, walked into the creek, squatted, pissed, splashed water on her crotch, climbed out of the water, slipped on her panties, her dress.

"You know, I believe Jill is right," she said. "The judge doesn't need any credit card spy system to know when a high voltage person is coming."

She walked with the doctor, up toward the cave. The girls were lying on the ground in front of what was left of the heads. On the cliffs, the ruins dripped blood. Jane got up, brought over a pair of underpants. "Here, Doctor." She held them out. A piece of flesh fell.

"I'll go into the cave, get your clothes," said Gwen.

"Jill, to say those bulls broke because I'm impure or blasphemous just isn't true. To put things in their proper perspective, all things that have an age are subject to the laws of time and change. Likely, those bulls were, of themselves, changing. That doesn't mean they should no longer be honoured; but, perhaps, should be honoured as we honour friends who have died. We don't die with our friends, but walk the path to our own time. Perhaps, the bulls were ready to die; you, loving them, held them past their time. Then you gave your love to me, the bulls were released, felt free to die."

Jill sat up. "You speak of release as if it were the most pleasurable thing in the world, like going to a party. Do you stop loving your friends to release them?"

"I don't stop loving my friends," said the doctor. He pulled his underpants on. Some horsemen were riding up through the woods.

75

The girls ran for the cave.

"Stay out," said Jill. "The cave's a holy place."

The doctor, alone outside, ran for a tree. The horsemen rode up. "What's that thing?" said Mr. Applegate.

"Looks like one of those ascension robes," said Mr. Prescott.

" 'Cept it's camouflaged, like a disguise," said Mr. Applegate. He looked around, pointed up, said, "He's in that tree."

"Think he's waitin' for the second coming?" Mr. Prescott asked. "What are you doing in that tree?" shouted Mr. Applegate.

"He's responsible for you, you ungrateful wretch," said Mr. Prescott.

"I'd beat the arse orf him," said the third man.

"Get out a that — " shouted Mr. Applegate.

"I'd beat the arse orf him," said the third man.

Whap went Mr. Applegate's whip on the doctor's thighs. The doctor gasped, said, "I was just - "

"Silence, miserable critter," yelled Mr. Applegate. Whap. "What do you know what's just." Whap. "This is just." Whap.

"I'd beat the arse orf him," said the third man.

Whap. Now you march yourself in front of us, straight up and down like a soldier marches, look neither right nor left, try any funny stuff and I'll tromp your guts out under my horse," shouted Mr. Applegate.

The fields passed, the cobblestone street, the wooden footbridge, the path to the stone building, a low door, a hall. "Go in there," said Mr. Applegate. "Go down those steps. Open an iron cage, Mr. Stubbs. I have a bird."

An old, bent man got up from his desk, opened an iron grill door. Clang.

Three men stood outside looking in, then walked away. Mr. Stubbs walked away. There was silence. Mr. Stubbs came back with a dish of beans and a tin cup of coffee. He stuck them through the grill. The doctor took them.

"Is this the usual dinner?"

Mr. Stubbs stood and stared. He sat at his desk.

"I say, is this the usual meal?"

"I speck you'll be here a long time, so 'twill avei:age out, or I wouldn't say this. On the average, I speak one word a day to prisoners."

The doctor ate. Mr. Stubbs took the dish and cup back, went up the hall. He came back, sat behind his desk, stared.

Officer Shorb and a big fat officer came in the doorway, said a word to Mr. Stubbs. Mr. Stubbs came, opened the iron door. Officer Shorb walked up. "Baliles, this is Officer Hughes."

Officer Hughes opened a notebook.

"I'll need a couple forms filled out, let's see, ah, by what name are you known, full name?" asked the fat officer.

"Albion Brandon Baliles."

"Are you known by any other names?"

"None."

"Where do you stay?"

"Seven one four Poplar Drive, Falls Church, Virginia."

"Is this your permanent home?"

"Yes."

"Place of birth?"

"Rochester, New York."

"Your age?"

"Thirty four."

"Previous arrests?"

"None."

"Now put your finger here. Now roll it this way. Now this finger. Now this finger. Yes, um hum, um um. Now the other hand. Now here. Um hum. Um um. Now here. Um hum. Um hum. Now thumb.

Um hum. That will be all. Yes, that's it. Thank you, Baliles."

Mr. Stubbs motioned with his hand, banged the iron door shut. Officer Shorb and Officer Hughes went up the hall. Mr. Stubbs sat staring. He got up, walked up the hallway. There was silence. Somewhere there were faint echoey sounds. Mr. Stubbs came back with Officer Shorb.

"You're wanted," said the officer.

Mr. Stubbs unlocked the grill door. Officer Shorb walked with Dr. Baliles through the dark corridor, up the hard stone steps, down the dark hall, opened the door to the room with the pews. The dim globes of light hung from the ceiling. There was the judge up front, one hand raised; a goggle like hemisphere, as large as a grapefruit, covered each eye. Mr. Whistler stood with pursed lips in the back left corner. The silent court waited on the judge who hovered over it, the bowl sized goggles glaring out over the many faces.

"Mr. Prosecutor," said the judge. "You may call your first witness."

Mr. Whistler pointed at Dr. Baliles.

"Will the defendant take the stand," said the judge. "We can dispense with the swearing in. The witness has already been sworn."

"What are you doing in court in your underdrawers, Bulleyes?" snapped Mr. Whistler.

"Baliles is the name. Dr. Baliles. I was down by the river — "

"Making a getaway, Bulleyes?"

"I was not."

"That is all, Bulleyes," snapped Mr. Whistler. The prosecutor walked toward the rear.

The judge said, "Does the defense wish to cross examine?"

Mr. Applegate sat in stony silence.

"Next witness," said the judge.

Mr. Whistler said, "Mr. Clive Prescott."

The clerk walked up. "Do you swear to tell the truth, the whole truth, nothing but the truth so help you God?"

Mr. Prescott sat down.

"Mr. Prescott," said Mr. Whistler, walking slowly toward the witness stand, his hands behind his back, "Tell the court. Where was the defendant, Bulleyes, when you saw him this morning?"

"Hiding in a tree."

Mr. Whistler raised his eyebrows, asked in a high surprised voice, "Hiding?"

"Well, if it were a cherry tree: I might have thought, picking cherries. I looked in the tree, didn't see nary a cherry."

"Um hum. What did you see?"

"This man here."

"Was there any other person with you when you discovered the defendant?"

"Mr. Will Took and Mr. Arthur Applegate himself, the defense attorney."

"When was the last time you saw the defendant?"

"I went with Mr. Applegate to lock the defendant in gaol. Mr. Applegate was afraid he might run away."

"The fact is, you saw Bulleyes running away, is that true?"

"Speck it is." Mr. Prescott nodded.

"No further questions."

"Does the defense wish to cross examine?" said the judge.

"I do not."

The judge said, "Mr. Whistler, you may call your next witness."

"Prosecution rests," said Mr. Whistler.

The judge said, "Mr. Applegate, you may present your witnesses."

"I call the defendant to take the stand."

"The defendant will take the stand."

Said Mr. Applegate, "Are you the same, had dinner with me yesterday?"

79

"Yes."

"What did we eat?" the attorney asked.

"Roast beef, Yorkshire pudding, corn, peas."

"How about before dinner?"

"Wine."

"What games did we play?"

"Chess."

"Who said checkmate?"

"Mr. Hardesty."

"Who else?"

"Your wife."

"He's the same feller. Only, I could have sworn his eyes were blue," said the attorney.

"My eyes are blue," said Dr. Baliles.

Mr. Applegate took a step toward the bench, "Would you have the court clerk please check the colour of the defendant's eyes for me, Judge Horsley."

"The court clerk may check, and enter into the court records, the colour of the defendant's eyes."

The court clerk went forward, looked. "They are brown, sir."

"Thank you, Mr. Sedgewick. No more questions," said Mr. Applegate.

"The prosecution may, if it wishes, cross examine," said the judge.

Mr. Whistler strode forward. "Why are you wearing those drawers in court?"

"Because I was down by the river - "

"Was it you, yesterday, looking at the creek?"

"Yes, I suppose so."

"Were you or no?"

"Yes."

"Why were you looking at the creek?"

"Because the bridge was out and — "

"Why were you looking at the creek?"

"Because the bridge — "

"It's the creek I'm talking about, Bulleyes. Why were you looking at the creek?"

"Because I couldn't get across — "

"Bulleyes, why were you looking at the creek?"

"Because I couldn't—"

"Get across, Bulleyes? Get across, Bulleyes, get across? — No further questions," shrieked Mr. Whistler. He walked to the back comer of the room.

"Has the defense any further witnesses?"

"None, Your Honour." Mr. Applegate passed his fingers through his short, wavy hair. "The defense rests."

"The prosecution rests," snapped Mr. Whistler.

"The jury will now retire to determine the verdict," said Judge Horsley.

The jury filed out of the room. Mr. Whistler stood in the back comer of the room, a vague frown on his face. People moved restlessly in the pews. Mr. Billup coughed twice, cleared his throat. As people twisted and turned, the pews squeaked, then there was silence. Somebody whispered. It was quiet.

The bailiff said, "Will the court please rise."

The jury filed back into the room. People were seated.

The judge banged his gavel. "Will the defendant please rise. Has the jury reached a verdict?"

A short man, with a bald head, stood up. Perched on his nose; rimless, octagon spectacles. "We have, Your Honour."

"How does the jury find the defendant?"

81

"Guilty, as charged."

The judge frowned. "Albion Baliles, you have been found, by a jury of your peers, guilty as charged. By the authority vested in me under the laws of the City of Waterford, I sentence you to a thousand years." He banged his gavel. "Officer, return the prisoner to his cell."

Officer Shorb led Dr. Baliles out of the room, down the dark hallway. A big fat officer, Officer Hughes, followed. Down the cold stairway they went, through the dark corridor; in, past the desk of Mr. Stubbs.

"We're back with your man," said the fat officer.

"Thank you, Officer Hughes." Mr. Stubbs got up, opened the iron grid door; indicated, with his hand, to enter. The cell door closed with a bang.

"Goodbye for a long time, Mr. Bulleyes," said Officer Shorb. "Say, Hughes, his eyes did look sorta bull like, at least — " His voice faded out as he went up the hall.

Mr. Stubbs sat behind his desk, staring.

"Mr. Stubbs. My eyes do feel kind of achy. How do they look to you?"

Mr. Stubbs sat and stared. There was silence.

"It's as if the whole world turned to stone," the doctor said.

Mr. Stubbs just stared. Mr. Stubbs got up, went out. Then there was no movement at all. Mr. Stubbs came back with a tin cup of coffee and a small dish of potato salad on which was a tiny sliver of ham. He handed them through the bars. The doctor ate. Mr. Stubbs took the dishes back through the bars; then, returned to his desk and sat.

"May I use the latrine?"

Mr. Stubbs pointed under the bed. There was a potty. The doctor pulled it out and sat. He looked at the wall to his left. There were scribbles, words, names, all over the dirty grey. Mr. Stubbs sat and stared.

The doctor got up and sat on the bed. "Do you empty it?"

"No." Mr. Stubbs sat.

A big fat man with a double chin came in.

Mr. Stubbs went out.

The doctor shifted his position. The fat man leaned back in his chair. "Do you empty this pot?"

"Before breakfast every day."

"Oh," said the doctor. He sat and looked at the grey wall.

"Say, if I may ask, what are those big goggles the judge wears?"

"They say they help magnify. But that's what they say. I don't know — First time I saw 'em."

"What may I call you?"

"I'm Dorsey. George, if you like."

"I'm glad you don't ration your words like Stubbs does."

"No ration. But as the years roll on, you'll find we have less and less to say to each other. It amounts to the same thing. A year or two from now, you'll be saying as few words to me as you do to Stubbs. Your only entertainment will be the comings and goings of wrongdoers who come and go in these other cells here. You, I'm told, won't be having comings or goings until it's feet first out."

"George, my head feels big, my eyes feel swollen."

"That's not odd. It's been a hard day for you." George nodded, "I've heard other convicts say that."

George sat and stared, half asleep. The doctor looked at the writing on the wall.

"I've never seen such a collection of vulgarities and obscenities. Lots of names."

"Old as the hills. Gaol's older than the country itself. Some famous I'm told. Some's been put there in my time."

"I can't see any historic names. No names I recognize. Let's see: Mel MacQueen; Morgan White; Buster Gilbreath; Hicks Lee; J. Farquhar; Slim Doory; Rich Byrd; hum, but then there're lots a Rich Byrds; Elbert Jones; petrified kitty shit; Howard Scruggs; Hamish

83

Ridgeway; Burl Wilson; Big Dave Bygraves; panic button push here; secret doorknob; Ralph Stackpole; Watkin Smiley; Fuzzy Markham; Hawk Hawkins; Fred Jones; Goon Sandidge; James Foxx; Homer Darby; Diamond Stickley; this I can't make out; something Randall; Oscar Messerschmidt; this one says Burnside, I think; Will Davies; grated elephant turds; the judge eats it; don't throw cigarette butts in the toilet; what are cigarette butts; Jack Wilderspin; some Meade; Ives; bullshit hole; Clement Ballard; Smokey Jones; Brook Gracie; Rocky Miller; Charlie Nickerson. Can't say they mean a thing to me. You know 'em?"

"Let's see. Most of them's from way back. Big Dave. He says he signed that half a century ago. He was the big white haired man, second row, at your trial. Hawk Hawkins I remember. That's a Darby from up country. Should be more than one signed. Fred Jones, that's last year. He stayed a year. There was a Foxx. There's Charlie Nickerson. Want to sign the register?"

"Me add to that bullshit? Certainly not."

"Suit yourself. But every name's legit. None recent got less than thirty days, or they got no pencil from me. No just restings signed in my time. And they got no pencil from Stubbs, I guess."

"Well, let me sign then."

"I figured some day or other you'd be writing something there."

George got up laboriously, walked over and handed the doctor a pencil, went back and sat down. Dr. Baliles signed his name on the wall. George sat, looked half asleep.

"What time is it?"

George looked at his watch. "Nearly nine o'clock." George sat. Time ticked away.

Jill was at the doorway. She put her fingers to her lips. She was naked except for her thin white gown, her sandals. Other girls were behind her in their gowns. Jill put a rope loop over George. Minnie wrapped his face in a rag. Sally Ann grabbed his gun. "Ulp ulp," yelled George through the rag. Connie, Becky looped another rope over George, wrapped it round and round down to his ankles. Jane got his keys, opened the cell.

84

"Come," she whispered.

They ran up the corridor, through a door on their right, down some dark stone steps. They walked through the dark; feeling, on their right, the iron grills of cells.

They came to a door, went through, down old stone steps to a narrow passage, entered a round tunnel, an old drain, walked through, out into the bright moonlight at the water's edge. They turned left, followed the creek bed, came to where the water spread out wide, stopped. The girls, the doctor, waded out, swam, walked up, into the dell, up under the cliff. There were the heads, rotten and stinking of death.

"We aren't mad at you anymore," said Sally Ann.

"We're really sorry," said Jill. "Really. We didn't know you."

Said Polly, "Like expecting something to go zip and it goes zap."

"Well, I'm a bit confused," said the doctor, "but it seems there's a pattern."

The girls stood, somewhat uncertainly, in a formless group near the doctor.

Some looked at the cave and the ruins.

Said the doctor, "I'm beginning to think my situation isn't all that good."

Said Polly, "You do understand, you do know."

Rhonda stepped up, "If you were to escape, I'm certain you'd be faster than us. Then we would — "

"I wouldn't do that. No," said the doctor, "I would never run from your ritual. Jill, this is your last ritual as high priestess I am thinking. What ever it is, we will share it and, even now, I feel I am floating into ritual."

The girls looked from one to another.

"We should never have let you go back to the court."

"But then I wouldn't have gotten to write on George's wall."

Alice pulled down the doctor's underpants. Jill kissed the doctor's chest, knelt and hugged his knees.

"Can we make you a crown of flowers? It wouldn't take us but a minute?" Jill asked.

"No Jill, not now. There will be plenty of time later for flowers."

Jill began to cry. "Flowers yes, later. Anything else you will want, at all." "Songs. Dances. That sort of thing. Of all the world's multitudes, why me?"

It's all so strange." He put his hands gently on Jill's shoulders, drew her to him.

Libby went up, put her head on the doctor's chest, hugged him tight. "I want to know. Will you tell me about dying?"

"Yes Libby. Dying is our step into the unknown. It is difficult usually, usually painful. Dying is part of life. If we spend one day dying, we probably spend thousands of days doing other things."

The doctor put an arm around Libby and pulled her close. "I guess what I wanted to know is, really, about death."

"Yes, there's a separation between the two. When a recognizable part of the living drifts into the unrecognizable, timeless unknown; that is death. However; whatever living spirit death might thrust us into, dying would likely be its worst feature. That usually, as we see, takes little time. Then, wherever the long future thrusts us, know that we will be loved and honoured in the hearts of those who care. That is why love is important. I haven't told you everything about death, or dying. There are wisdoms and understandings developed over a period of time. So ask me again and again. When you have worries, fears; Libby, come to me, come and know there is ever a place where you are honoured, loved." He kissed her hair, her forehead.

"I was dreaming we ran away together, I became the wife of a history professor," said Jill.

"Beautiful dream. But we won't do that, will we?"

The moon shone down on the dell making things bright.

The doctor looked up. "Oh my, time is running out. But there's still time and time to say goodbye and I love you very much, all of you.

All of you, and Gwendolyn also, have loved, served, must, dressed in white, continue to serve; by serving, have obligated yourselves to further service; this is the rule: but not an obnoxious rule to obey. There shall be a certain pleasure in it. The rules are few. I'll tell you this: Love freely where your heart is. The chiefest among you is to be Rhonda. It is she whom you may now address as High Priestess. Jill, my relations will want to know somewhat of what you have to tell. If you will, contact my nephews in Mobile, Kay and Randolf Campbell. But stay yet awhile. You will know when to go."

A rotten head fell with a plunk and left a dark hole. "Now it is time."

"Are you still Dr. Baliles?" asked Becky, doubtfully. "I was never more so."

The priestesses slipped out of their gowns. Jill pressed herself desperately in the doctor's embrace.

"May this moment never end," she said.

"Jill, with no limiting word or qualification, Jill, I love you. Only the past is never ending, is forever. You must step back."

Jill stepped back. The other girls, with tear stained faces, stood waiting.

The doctor said, "Be quick now. It is time."

"I'm nervous," said Connie. "Will it hurt you?"

"Think not of that now. Time, time is now. Step forward. Move." The doctor spoke with some impatience, some urgency in his voice.

"You must touch nothing above the shoulders. Keep that strictest rule," said Rhonda.

Becky's mouth was bright red. Jill had blood dripping out of the corner of her mouth. In the bright light of the moon, nearly full, the girls seemed a circle of flashing teeth, teeth bright in the moonlight.

"There is so much that is beautiful; the flowers, the moonlight, being in love. At last, yes, being in love," said the doctor.

The clouds passed by, passed overhead, passed over the moon.

"Thank you, thank you," said the doctor, perhaps to himself; indeed, almost as an afterthought.

And so ends the account of Mrs. Campbell. That is, Mrs. Kay Campbell; or, Jill Campbell, of Waterford. To which, she never returned.

THE LEGEND IN GOLD

A legend in gold. And he went into a valley. The birds sang there. The afternoon sun shone on the leafy boughs of the trees coating them in dusky gold. And the dark stream flowed beneath the trees sparkling here and there with bright specks of sunlight. There were fish in the stream and some trees bore the pink peach, some the golden pear. The man's hair fell over his shoulders, more golden than the pear and the man's skin also was golden. Short soft grasses there were and tall grasses also. And of flowers they were many. They were bright on the hillsides and on the lands, where the water flowed out from the trees, they burnt gold in the sunlight. Among great grey rocks, under the dark blue of the sky, the man sat on a rock. Overhead sailed puffy white clouds across the blue. Down the stream there floated a ship and it was all blue and white like the sky that day. And on the ship was the Snow God and in his hand was a black stick and the stick had holes in it so that the white light shimmered through. "This is a magic stick,:" said the god and he gave it to the man and the ship floated on, on down the stream. The man kept the stick with him. And he puzzled over it. The deer came down to drink. And there, did the herons flap long wings and dip and sink. Then came the silvery dusk. The breezes blew the tree leaves. The moon sent down its shower of silver on the evening dew. The night birds sang sweetly in the hills and the far hills answered the melody and morning came. Clear lemon washed the East. The clouds took on ripples of gold and all the birds were singing - some, for the dawning light; some, for the last flying clouds of night; some for the golden day to come. The sun rose. The clouds sailed through the sky, a fleece of white. And there were little pigs come to gather acorns under the leafy oaks. The wind sang in the trees his song of blue and white and sun patterns danced among the flowers. In the grass, the spiders spun their webs of dew jeweled fire. Against the rocks, always the brook sang. On the surrounding hills, among the blue flowered chicory, the mourning doves cooed their sweet sad song of golden Yesterday. The man took up the magic stick. He looked through the holes in it at the blue sky. And the sun was golden. And the bell trees dripped pale petals of their flowers. The clouds floated high over distant blue hills.

Again the ship, all blue and white like the day, was floating hugely down the brook all white sails, blue hull. And there, the White God. "Have you learned the magic of the stick?" asked the god. "Not I," said the man. "Then I will_tell it, you," and he whispered it to the man. "Ah," said the man. The wind tossed the trees and the White God sailed far away. A day passed, then another. The sun which rose over another blue and white day, found the man in another valley, on a green peopled with youths, blue eyed, and maidens, golden haired. They took his hands and had him join them in their singing.

They asked him the meaning of the black stick. The man thought and puzzled over what the god might have said. But the man could not tell them. Already he had forgotten.

The shadows got long and the children went away. The sun sank and the moon rose pale over the valley and the birds whistled far away. And the birds whistled far away.

The May Eve Picnic

The four aces had met in college, formed a singing group. Paul Hart, John Diamond, Mike Batt and Alfred Gardiner each, on stage, dressed as a playing card ace. Though their fame was small due to the limits of their ability, they remained good friends and, after college years, would meet on holidays to dine together and sing together their old songs. April Fools Day was honoured with a meeting, with April Fool songs and jests.

"You know, there is an ancient ruin near Moundsville where a ghost is said to appear every May Day Eve," said Paul.

"April Fool," said Mike.

"No. You can check that out," said Paul.

"It is a joke on the nonbeliever."

"Which is all of us," said John.

"List me as a nonbeliever with just a trace of the skeptic," said Paul.

"I would consider myself as very skeptical of there being any ghost, but I suppose that is still a type of skeptic," said Al.

"I would have said nonbeliever; but, really, pinned down," said Mike, "I should perhaps admit to a trace of uncertainty."

"Now what are we to check out?" said John.

"Why," said Paul, "the story that a ghost appears on every May Eve. By nonbeliever, I didn't mean nonbeliever of ghosts, but nonbeliever of the story as opposed to me telling an April Fool joke. I don't believe there are really any ghosts either, but this legend is, I assure you, taken quite seriously in that town."

"What ghost?" said Al.

"Now this," said Paul, "is the strange point. There is no agreement.

No two people seem to have seen the same ghost there. Also, many who have gone there have not lived to tell what they saw. Some have just vanished."

"Let us, then," said Al, "hold our next feast and sing-along on that very spot. Then we can see if any ghost appears."

"Or, when we next hear that story," said John, "we can laugh and say that we saw one May Eve when no ghost was there, or at least that we could see."

All thought this a great plan, a capital arrangement. Plans were made to take food, spirits and good voice to the center of that ruin, sing May Day songs and early European floral songs. On May Eve, at six o'clock, they would meet to eat and sing. May Eve arrived. Paul was there. John was there. They arranged the picnic table, a folding table of old wood, set it for four, but it was six o'clock. There was no Mike, nor was Al present.

"We did say six o'clock?" Paul asked.

"Yes. We talked about eight; but quite definitely, we agreed on six. I wonder if those two mixed up the time. It is nearly seven."

"Yes," said Paul.

"Allowing for tardiness, they should have been here by now."

The two looked at the ruins and the surrounding area. "That's why we said six," said John. "We wanted time to give the place a good look over before darkness set in."

Eight o'clock came and went. Then eight thirty.

"No, it was apparently not a mix up of the time. I must conclude something came up to delay them; too recently to inform us. Also, they must be traveling together."

Nine came and went. They walked to where they could see the old road. It came toward them from the town, then passed under the hill and away.

It was vacant. "Judas, I wish they'd hurry along. I know they'll be here, but when?" said Paul.

"It's twenty past nine already." The two turned back toward their table. There sat Mike.

"Oh, there you are. Where's Al? I thought you'd be together," said John.

Mike smiled and nodded. John and Paul sat down.

"The reason we wanted to start early, we wanted time to give the place a good look over," said Paul.

"We had lots of time, believe me, and we can tell you about it, but it's not seeing something for oneself. I suggest you stay, see it after sunrise." Mike shook his head.

"Then some other time. It is quite an interesting old ruin. Of course, we have St. John's coming up. We could come back."

"I like the idea of another picnic," said John. "But I would first want some assurance, we are together on the time. Here Paul and I have been since quarter till six. Now we must hope Alfred makes it by the witching hour."

"Where were those old graves they told us about?" Paul asked.

"I believe that little rugged area over there," John pointed, "is what they meant. We walked right by them a few minutes ago."

"You make it sound like ages ago. And it does seem like something we saw in a past age," said Paul.

"Now what in the hell is keeping Al?"

They heard a car coming down the road. It slowed. The sound stopped.

"That would be Al," said John.

"At quarter to ten, it would do well to be," said Paul.

They got up, went to where they could see down the trail. "Hello there," called a voice at the bottom of the dark trail.

Paul shouted, "Hello yourself. Where have you been, Alfred? It's going on to ten."

The figure, carrying a satchel, made its way up the trail, got to the top. Paul went on, "And John and I have been here since before six."

"Before six?" said Al. "I thought we agreed, eight o'clock."

"No," said John, "we quite definitely said six. Just you and Mike must have had earplugs in your ears."

"Anyway, running late though I was," said Al, "I do believe I would have made it by eight, but there was a wreck on the highway and stupid drivers couldn't go forward and wouldn't go back and all I could do was to sit and blow my horn in irritation, which you can bet there was of a plenty; then, finally —"

"But you weren't yourself injured?" asked Paul.

"There's my car down there, is it not?" said Al.

"But we can't see from here what shape it's in," said John.

Al took things from his satchel, spread them on the table. "See," he said. "Not a beer bottle broke. Have some."

They each opened a bottle. They lit candles.. Food was passed around.

"Let's sing," said Paul. They sang songs old and new, some ancient. They raised their mugs on high; sang May songs, love songs, songs about flowers, college songs, drinking songs, songs to gods and goddesses of drink and flowers.

"Here's to things done just for the hell of it," said Paul.

"Here's to the mother of Mercury," said John.

They drank. "Boy, what a great May Day," said AL.

"Yes, it turned out very well," said John.

They sang and drank and sang. As light touched the east, said Paul, "We must be off to our breakfasts."

"I don't believe," said Al, "we've ever sounded better."

"Right," said Paul. "Those songs would, I believe, have gotten cheers if they had been sung that way on a concert stage."

"All in all, in spite of a slow start, we had fun," said Al.

"Take care driving back."

They headed down the trail. The east was touched with colour. In the next town, John parked at a small inn. He found a table, ordered breakfast.

Paul came in and joined him. "For a start, I could use coffee," he said.

"We did sound pretty good," said John.

"And," said Paul, "our reason for being there. We spent the entire of May Eve till the very crack of dawn and the only spirits we saw were those from our own bottles."

"So much for ghosts," said John.

"Yeah, we knocked that ghost thing in the head.," said Paul.

A newspaper man brought in a stack of papers, put them on the breakfast room counter. John went up and bought one. On the front page was a picture of a wreck.

"There's Al's wreck," said John, pointing to the picture.

Paul borrowed the paper, looked at the wreck. "Look, that's Mike's car."

"Are you sure?" John took back the paper.

"You know, it is. That explains why we didn't see him drive up. He got a lift. How did he get back? With Al?"

John continued to look at the picture. "Oh look, Paul. That's Mike still in the car."

Paul took the paper, looked hard at the picture. "John," he said, "Mike never walked any place. See?"

Paul took back the paper. "Oh John, this is awful." Then his eyes went down to the text, read, "Driver died at the scene of the crash. There were no passengers."

"The give away," said John. "There's his card on the windshield." He tapped his finger on the car on the paper Paul held.

"But that," said Paul, "isn't his card. That one would have been Al's."

"We'll need to go be what help we can. Try to call his family. Poor Mike. I wouldn't mention last night to any of them. As I recall, he sang pretty well, didn't he?"

"My impression was, he did. And we'll need to get hold of Alfred," said John.

"Yes. Yes, we should," said Paul. "I wonder what possessed him to switch cards. Waiter, I'd like coffee over here please."

"I'd like my coffee too," said John.

WELLS ROAD

On a Sunday, when the weather was warm, Don and Willa would begin early in the morning, take a long walk; then, come back to Willa's house after sunset. Willa lived in a red brick house on a street of brick houses, most of them red, near the center of town. On this street, the houses were two and three story, their walls almost touching, and all had tiny front yards that separated them from the mossy brick sidewalk.

The sun was just rising as they finished a breakfast of coffee and cold cereal. It was bright, but cool for a St. John's day, which day it was. The two of them put on light jackets and began their walk. Over the damp brick sidewalk, under dark leafy trees, they walked, to a street of old stores and businesses with, here and there, a ruined vacant building. Then, down a side street they walked where the stores were even older and more were vacant and boarded up. Then there were houses jammed together, some with store fronts on their bottom floor. They walked toward the outskirts of town, down numbers of residential streets, many with groups of stores at their comers with their ancient architectural styles. Beside the larger streets that led to well kept suburbs, there were run down streets and alleys which led to factory districts, warehouses, shacks, or rubble strewn, wooded lots. The street Don and Willa now were on seemed to be one of the latter. It was an alley-like street through old houses in poor condition. The name they noticed was Cheapside Street and they had never been on it before. Don and Willa were always surprised to find themselves on such a street. There were, however, a great many such around the fringes of the city and in its out of the way sections. The houses became more separated; old stone; old brick; some, dilapidated frame. At a cross street, Cheapside became Wells Road. The lots, mostly vacant now, were covered, many of them, with rubble, ruins, or patches of trees. The few old brick buildings were dilapi dated and there seemed no people about. They crossed rails of a once used railroad, walked on. An old lady in a faded blue dress sat on a roofless porch. A couple of dirty kids played in the dirt and an old hound came toward Don and Willa and barked a couple of times.

"Don't go down that street," they heard the lady shout. Willa jumped.

"Oh, she's talking to her kids," said Willa.

"Or her dog." On they walked past empty lots, past houses in ruins. The road had become rough cobble stones with cracks and holes out of which grew weeds. The sun had become hot on their backs. A couple of skinny dogs came from a ruined foundation, followed them barking now and again. The dogs slowed, stopped. They continued to bark. Don and Willa walked on, left the barking dogs in the distance. The road had become more and more a weed filled trail.

"This road seems to be running out," said Willa.

"We could tum back," said Don. They turned around, started back. When they turned, they noticed the dog barks sounded as if they were in a barrel, then seemed to be getting not closer, but more distant. Then they faded completely out. Don and Willa walked back along the road.

"It looks different," said Willa.

"Different perspective," said Don. They walked on.

"No," said Willa. "Somehow we've gotten turned around. We aren't on the same road. See?"

"I'm beginning to," said Don. "This is spooky."

They walked on. They came to some very ancient stone buildings.

"We'd better tum around." They turned around, retraced their steps. As they came to the place where they had turned, they could hear the distant barking of dogs. But now, as they walked, the dogs became more distant. They passed a tumble down building, lines of trees that seemed to indicate where buildings had once stood. Again they turned around. The lines of trees were different and they didn't come to the vacant building they had just passed a hundred yards back.

"We'd better turn back around," said Don. They turned around, walked a couple of hundred yards. Here was the tree near which they had turned. They continued on.

"This is scary," said Willa.

"It seems we're in some sort of trap," said Don, "But this road must lead to someplace."

"We haven't gotten to any wells yet," said Willa.

The road was now a trail over wooded hills, past rocky weed covered fields. There were places where farm lanes seemed to lead off.

"I'm tempted to walk up one of these lanes," said Don.

"I'd like to see a farmhouse first," said Willa. "Or they could be the ultimate trap."

They walked on. They came to a place below the crest of a hill where a dirt road seemed to cross the road which they were on.

"Here's where we get off this road," said Don. "Right or left?"

"Right, I think," said Willa. "I'm still scared."

The two travelers turned off their road, followed the dirt trail, over hills and through valleys. From a hilly area, they could now see buildings, but couldn't be sure what they were.

"Some town," said Don. "I hope it's one in our world."

They walked on. On past wooded hills. They came to a country road, turned right and followed this. Here and there, back from the road, they saw farm houses. They came to a crossroads where there was a small grocery store, a couple of houses and a filling station. The two stopped in at the grocery store, bought some cold meat and buns.

"How does one get to the city?" asked Don.

Said the grocer, "Go straight ahead, take the right fork till you come to Churchtown. From there you will see signs on the main road out of town. It will take you right in. Say where's your car?"

"We don't have one," said Don.

"Then how're you gonna get there? Walk?"

"Yes."

"Well I'm damned," said the grocer.

THEY HAVE IT LOCKED UP
IN CINCINNATI

I walked along a dark, narrow street that seemed extra dark because of the dark overcast that filled the sky. The days, lately, had seemed to vary between dark and darker; the darker, filled with intervals that stopped short, stopped just this side of being hard rain. The dark days had seemed to go on forever, but I had to remember that this was Baltimore and that its location, a region where warm, moist air off the Gulf Stream encountered the cool air masses from off the high hills and mountains of Frederick County, should lead one to anticipate a great many clouds. This was one of those darker days and, as habitual on such days, a fine drizzle commenced, making walking the less pleasurable. A city bus rumbled up the street, stopped, and I got on it. It wasn't going in my direction, but would go to the end of the line, tum around and, after a journey through winding streets, eventually arrive at the apartment building where I was staying. We rumbled down the street, passing buildings of damp, dark brick and now and again a figure under a black umbrella. The day grew darker. In darkness we turned around at the end of the line.

Heading now back uptown, we picked up a man in a shabby dark coat and dripping felt hat. He took a seat in front of me, sat mumbling to himself. The bus made a turn.

"You should have made that turn wider. We'll end up payin' to replace curb stones," said the mumbling man, a bit louder than his former mumbling, perhaps speaking to the driver.

The driver gave no indication of having heard.

The bus rolled on and the critical man mumbled to himself from time to time.

The bus stopped, picked up an elderly woman, started up.

"Wait, there's another comin' might want to catch the bus. What fools the city hires nowadays," said the critical man.

The bus driver's ears reddened. He stopped.

"There's only one person can drive this bus at a time. Any more such remarks from you, and I'll wait for you to get out of it."

The bus rolled on, picked up here a man; here, two men. It rolled down the road.

"See how this bus jerks when it rides? When I was young, bus drivers could make it run smooth. Yes, bus drivers back in those —"

The bus stopped. The bus driver stood up, came back to where the man sat. "All right, you're out of it, mister."

He reached in his pocket, handed the man some change. "Here, take another bus to where the Hell you're going, but you and I can't ride this one together."

The man got up, got off. As it was near my place, I got off, too. Night had come and an end to the drizzle. Ragged clouds were swimming through the sky and, to my amazement, there was the moon. My fellow rider from the bus, walking in front of me, looked up. He shook his fist at the moon.

"You old bastard. You wrinkled up son of a bitch. Come down here, and I'll punch you silly. Kick your dog, too, you bastard. I know you've got it locked up out there in Cincinnati. You old bastard. You old bastard up there."

He shook his fist at the moon, the moon now gone behind dark cloud masses. I passed him and went on to my place.

It was a morning a couple of days later. It was a gray day with a damp mist: still no sun. I, with an arm full of groceries, waited in a damp queue of shoppers in a grocery store which sat on a comer near my place. I heard a shopper a couple of people ahead of me mumble to the sales clerk.

"I hear it's locked up in Cincinnati."

"Yes, at the National Guard Armory," said the clerk.

Then in front, a customer with a bag of groceries in her arms, an old lady, looked out the window.

"Sure is gray and nasty. Hope it won't last forever."

"No telling," said the clerk.

He went back to adding prices, the lady's in front of me, then my groceries were totaled up. I paid, strolled out onto the dirty, damp sidewalk.

A couple of days later, still under a gray sky, I stood at a bus stop. This was the busy Wharves District, and a few others waited at the stop with me. We waited in silence for a few minutes. Then a man spoke.

"This goes on and on."

"I hear it's out in Ohio," a lady said.

"Lot of good it does them," said a short, fat man. "They have it locked up in Cincinnati."

"So I understand, at the National Guard Armory," said another man.

"So we're led to believe," said the short fat man.

Just then the bus came.

Later, back home, I thought to myself, "What a foolish rumor. I wonder how it ever got started."

Having the time, I thought it might be fun to personally put an end to that extravagant supposition, to take myself to Cincinnati, investigate that National Guard Armory. I packed a small satchel, went down to Camden Station. When the train to Cincinnati pulled out from the station, chugged over the rails under the sky filled from end to end with dark clouds, I was on it.

The next day, in Cincinnati, in a cloud of steam, we pulled into the station. I dismounted from my coach and, satchel in hand, walked through the passengers on the platform, walked up to the central part of the station; a huge, dome-like room where stone mosaics depicting working people looked down from the walls. I walked to the information counter.

"Can you direct me, please, to the National Guard Armory?"

"There is no National Guard Armory in Cincinnati," said a thin-faced, studious looking man in horn rim spectacles.

I walked away, saddened by the thought that I had made a futile trip; but, somehow, it didn't seem right, a city that size with no armory. I went to the concession stand, asked the stout, gray-haired lady there, "Do you know where the National Guard Armory is?"

"Certainly, I know where the National Guard Armory is. Go out to Dalton Street, go left. Take a right on Kenner Street. Up a block. You can't miss it. It sits between Kenner and Flint."

I went down, out the Dalton Street exit, walked up to Kenner Street, walked up Kenner. Looking back, I saw the station squatting there; a grotesque, half moon of stone, as if some giant Eskimo igloo, rendered in stone, had been sliced in half. But, looking forward, I saw no National Guard Armory. I walked up the street, as I was directed, and there was nothing there, nothing except old bricks, old stones and rubble. There was no National Guard Armory. The wind blew in the weeds and in the cold, dead grass in that muddy, weed and rubble filled waste beyond which hovered a clutter of broken and falling buildings, half buildings and roofless walls of old brick. There was no National Guard Armory. And certainly there was no sunshine.

BELLTOWN TO LINCOLN

The dark road sloped slightly upward toward the bay bridge. To my right, past the white guard rail, the tufty grass bank dropped off, leveled out to a fence bordering a parallel road. Ahead, the steel blue struts of the bridge; dark, shiny in the morning. The road at the right bent away, and here were mud spattered cement spaces where buildings had been, grass and weed growing in cracks and around edges. Now, lower down, as I walked upward; a wide, reddish roadway of worn brick, rusting rails of an extinct railroad in its center, ran toward the bridge. At its side, a few silvery semi trucks parked and more silvery semis at these crumbling, smoky brick buildings: warehouses I think: and some yellow and black trucks with streamlined fronts. I walked on: a brick alley: some more old buildings, ornate and tumble down, jammed closely together. This must be the last remains of the old section of Belltown. The brown pebbly sidewalk glistened in the sun in front of me. I was catching up with a slender young woman. She carried a large grocery sack - filled, perhaps, with groceries. As I walked behind her, I swung my tridocent back and forth, snug in its leather case and finely set for the light analysis which I had on the agenda for that day. To the front, over a metal grid sidewalk, rose the bridge steeply. Below, an old brick road ran under the bridge. Beside it, shrubs and marsh grass. Here, the muddy flats along the bay. Some leggy birds walked on the mud. On the metal grids I walked, walked up beside the thin young woman.

"I'll carry that sack for you if you'll just hang onto this little leather case for me."

"Whew," she said, "I sure would thank you. My arms are about to give out." We exchanged. Some pigeons flew out of the bridge structure to our left and crossed in front of us.

"What's in this little old case?"

"It's a tridocent."

"I don't know what that is?"

"It measures light."

"Can I look at it?"

"Please, no. It's sensitive to light and needs to be covered."

"Aw, one little peek?"

"Please don't open it."

"Just one peek?"

"Please, no."

Ripples of cloud hung in the bright sky overhead, over the struts of shiny dark steel. The bridge rose up, cast its crooked shadows on the wavy bay waters far below. Beyond these patterns, the waters stretched bright out to the sky. Way to the right, across the bay, the bright buildings of Clearview cut irregular patterns at the top of a hill. To the front, the tall buildings of Lincoln. There. She opened it. A month's work of settings shot to Hell. I just threw her damned groceries over the side, or whatever they were. She threw my tridocent over. Below me glistened the dazzling blue mounds of cut glass. On the bright mirror over me was caught the jagged white. The transparent lacework of bridge rose, shiny bright. On the bright mirror was Lincoln in cut crystal of amethyst and emerald and dark jet and cut diamond and aquamarine. Amethyst, emerald and aquamarine in shattered lightnings and dark pits displaying inward angles of shiny dark. Overhead, waves of electric brightness took off the top of the sky and the jagged white bit downward, bit downward on the transparent top of the bridge. Toward Lincoln, the prism sidewalk stretched long and bright. And my spirit shadow got shorter and shorter as it drifted onward toward those caves of voided light.

MR. FORSEY GOES TO A SHOW

It all began with the carnival coming. It was in the area at the time the county fair was to commence; so, as there was plenty of space, it was thought wise to invite them to come to the city and set up next to the Fair grounds. The city was Frederick; a small, farm town of a city set in farmland and farms all around went up to the city's edge, its pillars and old brick walls. So, coming out of the city, the fairgrounds were bounded on the left by farm buildings and a silo, so the crowds went past the silo and between farm buildings to get to the carnival set up on the farm's land; so that the carnival had some privacy which seemed, a secretness. The parade to the fairgrounds was set for August 19th, Frederick's wine fest, and the carnival was ready. Certain elements of the parade continued on down the path to the carnival, a circle of tens and platforms set a round at Ferris wheel and a number of strange rides, and a crowd came that way carrying their balloons and cotton candy. Loud band music drifted over from the fairgrounds. Barkers were shouting to draw crowds this way and that. At the end of the muddy path, past the first attractions; a ring toss for a prize off a shelf of stuffed animals and such; a photograph tent where one could stick his head through any of a selection of monsters, some of which displaying sex organs; a body paint tent where one could get design on as much of one's body as one wished; was a short row of dark tents pushed back into clumps of tall, scraggly weeds and summer flowers: Queen Anne's lace, goldenrod and chicory behind which were the dusty leaves and pale pink flowers of tall Joe Pye weed. There were four in the row; all, of a dark charcoal grey. The first belonged to a hippy candle maker. One could buy from selection of fancy candles or, with the help of a long haired, bushy bearded man, one could make his own candles.

The second tent belonged to the carnival's magician and inside were books and a number of other things one could buy. The third was the voodoo tent. Inside, a tarot reader gave a voodoo slant to her tarot readings. Then the fourth tent, longer than the others, was the

Mr. Forsey Goes to a Show

mirror tent. If modern technology had reached Washington, some miles down the road; it had not become widely known about in the area of Frederick; so, many there were interested in seeing what was there advertised as the latest in light technology. Inside the tent it was dark. Then, suddenly, thin fingers of light flashed and swirled around one as one walked along the rope bound passageway. One walked forward through the faintest white twilight as light forms took shape, changed, shimmered, went out, were replaced by others; then, at the far end of the tent, all lights and colours seemed pulled into a pit of darkness. Then in darkness, one followed the rope path, made his exit. As he reentered the bright summer day; his eyes, certainly, would still be swirling with the swirling light forms inside even if he had drunk none of the beverage which was the theme of the festival and he would likely be too giddy to stretch his legs in a straight line to the next attraction.

Edred Forsey was one of the few people in the city of Frederick who wasn't particularly interested in the Frederick County Fair. A dark haired architect a shade past forty, he had told his wife that he had no interest in going and beside, he had financial reports that required his attention. So, as usual, he went to his office. But when there, he found that his secretary had already done the reports. They looked quite right and all he needed to do was sign them. He looked out his window at the people below, all going to the county fair. It was true, fat hogs and fancy show chickens hadn't much appeal for him, but he did want to see what the schools had done with their science projects. And he had the time. He put on his hat, walked down the stairs to the old, dusty street, followed the crowd to where the street became a lane which led into the fairgrounds. The crowd was colourful, as it had become a custom to dress in styles colonial or earlier. And many of the people there in their usual dress would have needed little or no change to be in Colonial style clothes. Amish and hippies made additions to the variety of clothes one saw. Amish cooks and craftsmen were a traditional part of the county fair, but hippies were a colourful addition.

Mr. Forsey passed the dog show for which he had little interest. He passed where the tug of war was to take place, police against firemen, for which people were beginning to gather. He was interested in the flower tent. Florists showed a real art in their flower arrangements and displays. He went in the tent. Band music was suddenly softened by the canvas walls. On tables around the walls artistically displayed flower arrangements stood elegantly in the diminished light. Then, the next room, a waterfall around which was a colourful garden. The sign said "Created by Goebels of Wheaton". Then into a room, a formal dinner setting, the setting all in black, white and silver so that it gave the impression of being a picture by a master painter, one versed in Cubist art.

Mister Forsey walked into the next room in the center of which was a black wooden coffin, plain but with a high gloss, and this served as a center for a flamboyant masterpiece constructed of flowers. A neat sign informed the public that the sponsor of the display was the Werner Chambers Co., Rockville. Mister Forsey walked around the front of the coffin, walked out into a vestibule where women behind a counter were selling wicker baskets, bird houses and pots of herbs and flowers and on the counter were flyers from companies who had contributed to the show. Mister Forsey went out where sunlight fell on the milling crowds. He walked up the sawdust covered path, past where clowns at the pony rides were entertaining, toward the school projects tent.

Around that tent were crowds of children waiting to enter. One look at those lines changed Mister Forsey's direction. He took the muddy, rutty path between the paintless grey farm buildings to where the carnival was set up. He had little interest in the first tents he passed, but stopped at a sign which said "Hilliard Horton Mirror Light House" The low key wording on the sign made him curious. No mention was made of a fabulous or magical show. He paid for a ticket and went in.

Yes, it was good science, reflected beams of light doing what one might have thought light could not do. And the pulsing threads of light were in constant motion so that the shifting, flashing worlds which quickly changed, one for another, gave an out of body experience which young people would have called a trip. So the audience would have been gotten word of mouth and an overly verbose sign would have been considered trite. Mister Forsey followed the rope to the rear where light forms were sucked into a blackness: a black pit. He looked at the vanishing lights. The pit seemed also to eat the phantom twilight which seemed to hover about all the other lights. The darkness seemed to pull light from his eyes, so that seeing seemed observing light retreating into darkness. He wondered if those strange lights had damaged his eyes; but, as he followed the rope on around, he found, with relief, his could see the light images. Only, outside the tent, the things he saw seemed to contain a darkness, as if the colour in them were fleeing away from him. To him, that gave the day a darkness while the sun seemed shining as brightly as ever. He walked on. A group of people at the next tent were watching balls being thrown at tenpins which were set up at the back of the tent. He moved up to the group. A woman there looked over at him, moved away, walked away from the tent. A young farmer and his wife looked over at him, moved quickly away from the tent. The others there turned to look at him, look into his dark eyes below the brim of the dark grey fedora. They all walked quickly away. The man with the ball looked back at him, threw the ball. The ball hit the tarp short of the tenpins. The man walked off. Mister Forsey wandered down to where a crowd was waiting at the sword swallower tent. As he approached, one by one, people looked over at him. Each, with a startled look, or look showing discomfort, moved away. Mister Forsey walked to a crowd where food was being sold. He went into the crowd to see what the food was.

"Those eyes drill a hole into your head," said a man.

"They suck your brain out through your eyes," said another.

Someone nudged a man. The man looked back, jumped away, moved quickly off followed by a number of others.

Mister Forsey left that area, went to the path between the grey buildings, hurried over toward the county fair. A group coming toward him on the path looked into his eyes, turned around and hurried the other way. Mr. Forsey walked toward the school projects tent. He merged with the crowd until in front of him he came upon a man in a yellow hard hat. The two men, tall men, faced one another. To Mister Forsey, that man seemed to have no brain at all, to be a muscular robot. Under the hard hat, the face became contorted, the man turned, looked to the right, to the left. People looked at his face, fell on their knees, on their backs. The yellow hat stomped on the heads of people on the ground, kicked the faces of others, those bent over or kneeling. People fled before the yellow hat, ran into crowds not yet caught up in the panic. The yellow hat kicked backs., tore at people's faces, tore throats out. Some people fled toward Mister Forsey, saw him, stopped dead in their tracks, fled to the right and left, out into the fields. To the rear, Yellow Hat had run into the fields. Somewhere, a siren was blowing. Security men crossed the fairgrounds, ran in the direction which they had seen Yellow Hat go. Then from the right, Mister Forsey saw Yellow Hat coming toward him. The face below the hat seemed not human, but covered with deep, red and blue ridges; seemed more the face of a mandrill. The mouth and jaw, huge and heavy, looked as if they could rip off a man's leg.

Before he got to Mister Forsey, the yellow hat turned, ran back into the fields from which it had come. Sirens were blowing. Medics from the aid tent were treating injured people. Mister Forsey turned and left the fairgrounds.

Mister Forsey went home. His wife did not want to hear about the fair. She had a headache, went to bed. The next day, she vanished. That day, Mister Forsey read the paper, read that the police had shot an insane man, that a Mafia figure had been seen at the county fair. That week, Mister Forsey's secretary called to say she wouldn't be back. After that, nothing seemed to go right. Mrs. Forsey was found in the Monocacy.

ART FOR THE WALTERS

The infantry, the infantry
They drink up all the beers
The infantry, the infantry with dirt behind their ears.
The cavalry, artillery and combat engineers
Could never beat the infantry
In 50,000 years —
They say old sergeants love to drill
Until they fade away
They say old corporals love their stripes
And that ain't hay.
They say old privates love their beer
Three times a day
They say old soldiers never die
They just fade away.
Never die, never die, never die, never die
They say old soldiers never die
They just fade away.
You gotta get up, you gotta get up
You gotta get up in the morning.
You gotta get up, you gotta get up
You gotta get up I say.
Tramp, tramp, tramp the boys are marching
Soupie soupie without a single bean
You're in the Army now, you're not behind a plow.
You'll never get rich by digging a ditch
When Johnnie comes marching home again
Hooray, hooray, when Johnnie comes marching home again.
We're here because, we're here because, we're here because
We're here so here we are and here we are and here we are
Again
The coffee in the Army they say is mighty fine.
It looks like old tobacco juice and tastes like turpentine.

It's lights out now.
We have lights out with the bugle
Softly blowing   We march, march away, the long weary day
They say old soldiers never die, they just fade away.

Sergeant Beckwith stood in his foxhole, scanning the areas forward and to each side.

"Hello," said a voice behind him. He turned, saw a shining man, obviously an officer. Somewhat disconcerted, he saluted.

"See any evidence of Germans out there?" the officer asked.

"I think there's a trench full of them up that away, sir," the sergeant pointed, "You sure did get behind me quickly, sir. I sure didn't hear you comin'."

"Quite true. I'm Major Halstead, a Lamar S. I. Fellow. We've come up with something. Energy Projector. I'm wearing this extra one here. Put it on. This here in front, this in back. Now slip this little old suit here. Let's try for that knobby hill behind us. O.K. Look at your projector. That is your coordinate controle. Turn it so that your dial reads zero zero zero zero zero zero zero wunt thuree niner hater niner forwor six niner seven seven thuree. Got it? Now. Put your finger on the green button. Press down." The major disappeared. Sergeant Beckwith pushed the button.

The sergeant found himself standing next to the major. To his left, a couple of dark, broken, partly burnt trees rustled their sparse leaves in the slight breeze. Left of him, over the dark barren hills, the sun hung large and red in the graying sky.

"Easy wasn't it?" said Major Halstead. "Yes, there's that trench you spoke of Let's try for that." The major puzzled for a minute over a Rand range finder, replaced it in a pocket called a watch pocket. "A pocket of that size, in that location, in the britch of early Merekins, would have housed a watch. You know what that is? A spring operated time telling device. I've seen a couple of them. Highly inaccurate contraptions. I can't see how they could possibly have been of use to anyone. But people of that day had no feel for time position."

The wind rustled the tree leaves. The major searched the entire front with a small scope. The sun sank lower.

"Remember, that trench isn't under our cover shield. If there are no German: be as silent as possible," said the major. "And double check my scan."

"Yes, sir." Sergeant Beckwith got out his Halprinscope and he and the major searched the flat area, the bare earth and scorched grass to the front. Then, further on. the partly observable trenches among piles of earth and torn up ground. Further away and to the right, they checked the piles of bricks and caved in walls of a ruined village Then, out beyond, checked the low hills on which were patches of shrubs and trees; ai these, graying with the graying northern sky.

"O.K.," said the major, putting his scanner on his belt, "Set your dial to zero zero zero zero zero zero zero wunt forwor two niner fiyive forwor seven thuree six ze count. Now, finger on button. When I disappear, push." The major disappeared.

Sergeant Beckwith pushed. He stood at the end of a wide trench in which stoodod a couple of Germans; one pointing his lazorat at a Merekin; the Merekin, a long thin man with a scar on the side of his face, lying on his back at the bottom of the trench. Everything looked hazy and insubstantial. A large trunk, old and dusty, was in the trench beyond the head of the Merekin. The sun hung, a dull red.

The major appeared beside the sergeant, asked, "What is your setting?"

The German, with the lazorat in his hand, turned. A beam of light shot through the major.

"You see, we aren't all here," explained the major to Sergeant Beckwith. "My setting," said the sergeant, "is two zero zero zero."

"That's it," interrupted the major. "My apologies, sergeant; my fault, plus the fault of this idiotic language, having two words meaning the same thing. Set your dials, zero zero zero zero zero zero zero wunt thuree niner hater niner forwor six niner seven seven thuree."

The Merekin stood up, the Merekin with the scar running down across his cheek, crawled out of the trench. "Much obliged, sir," he said. He walked behind the sergeant and the major. The trench was bathed in the red light of the sunset.

"Got it?" asked the major. "Push your button."

The sergeant pushed. Back on the knobby hill, the sun resting on the low distant hills, flooded red light all over the countryside.

"Now try that trench setting again without the superfluous two. Those front knobs are anticipation settings. Correct your reading for the trench. It should read zero zero zero zero zero zero zero wunt forwor two niner fiyive forwor seven thuree six zero count. Dial set? Wait till I — "

The sergeant accidentally pushed the button. The Germans laughed. There was a flash and a beam of light struck the center of the shirt of the scar faced Merekin who was lying in the trench. A burned, charred spot appeared on the shirt. The Germans picked up the Merekin, opened up the trunk and stuffed him in.

"Save us some digging, ya?" said the German with nothing in his hand.

"Ya", said the German with the lazorat. "Run up a gortmiller and scan the area, then we'll go." The Germans laughed.

The major appeared. There was a flash. The one, then the other German, stood burned to a crisp, fell over.

"Got damn it to Hell, sergeant, I said wait," said the major. "I was exchanging my blaster for a ray gun cause I saw the Honk in the trench, and the box too, and I didn't want to damage him or the perishable merchandise. I just prayed to God they didn't realize there was a change in your status and fire again. You didn't even have a weapon in your hand, Got damn it to Hell. Now, where is that Honk?"

"Right here, sir," said the Merekin, a tall, skinny, bent, scar-faced fellow that looked like a straightened out coat hanger.

The major looked behind him. "Good," he said. "Here, let me have a look at that box." He jumped into the trench.

The sun set and the sky was darkening.

"Let's see: 'Art object To be sent to Goebels National Gallery of Art, Numburg, by order of General Gerhardt Vasannan.' Just fine. We'll redirect this little old art object." The major got out a lazorat, set the dials, crossed out General Vasannan's order and wrote, "Send to Walters Gallery of Art, Baltimore, by order of Major Everette Halstead, Lamar SJ." He got two cards from his hip pocket, wrote some information on them. "What is your name, soldier," he asked.

"Private Wallace D. Culpepper ADNOMRUTI, sir." "And yours, sergeant?"

"Sergeant Howard 0. Beckwith OURAVTZBC, sir."

The major held up the cards. "I have two week passes to Baltimore. Your job; deliver the trunk to Dr. Rhodes of the Walters. He'll sign your passes. Sergeant, if you'll give me back my uniform and projector. Thank you. I'm going to give you special cover which will last Jong enough. But go under the general cover as quickly as possible. Then clear through your nearest C.P. Enjoy Baltimore."

The sergeant and the private got into the trench, hauled the trunk out. The major took out his Schick Wilkinson, pointed it, like a Jong thin flashlight, at the horizon. The sergeant and the private carried the trunk between them. Schick balls of fire stood on the hills behind them blasting and burning the trees. Then, balls of fire above the first balls. Then another row above those. The two carrying the trunk walked as quickly as they could. A great boom shook the air and ground. They walked faster. Another boom. Another boom. A clap of thunder and the balls of fire vanished. A huge clap of thunder and the sky seemed to waver and shake. A sheet of flame covered the ground all over the area which they had vacated.

"Where's the Major?" the private, with some concern, asked.

"He was back long ago. Perhaps he's in Baltimore by now," Sergeant Beckwith told him.

"Incredible if it would be true," said the private. "I could hardly believe that. The two carried the trunk up past the knobby hill.

Beyond the hill were rising and falling meadows. They crossed a meadow to a gully, found themselves on a torn up country road. The road turned right, down a grade. The sergeant indicated they were to take the path to their left. The path led to a passage under a camouflage net, led into a C.P. bunker. A corporal sat at a desk. In the left corner sat a sergeant scanning his perception chart, the chart which informed the bunker of anyone approaching. The corporal looked up from his reports, received their passes, listed them on a report form.

"I'll have a hellis run you men to a jet port. What's your outfit, private? They'll need to be notified."

"I'm Fifth Battalion of Third Regiment, Fourth Company, Fifth Platoon. That's Fifth Brigade. The Fourth Dragoon of Seventh Corps."

"We're all Fourth of Seventh Corps here," said the clerk. He handed the passes back, pointed to the right rear. "Go through that passage. Get Private Henley off his ass."

Sergeant Beckwith and the private lifted the trunk and started for the passage. "Couldn't you find a substitute for me and let me stay here?" said Private Culpepper in a whiny voice. "That there box gives me the creeps, I don't mind telling yuh."

"You know the answer to that," said the sergeant as he backed into the passage. "You're on orders same as me."

They passed between dark sandbags, came out in an open area. Two privates stood talking under the rotary blades of the nearest of three hellis's.

The sergeant called, "Private Henley is to take us to a jet port. You two help us load this on his hellis."

The privates came over, grabbed corners of the trunk, carried it over and hoisted it on board. The private next to the sergeant got a form from his pocket, wrote on it, gave it to the sergeant. Sergeant Beckwith signed it, climbed on board. The private, then Private Culpepper climbed up. The sergeant sat next to Private Henley; Private Culpepper behind them sat on the box. They flew up. The sergeant looked back. There sat Private Culpepper; dark eyes, concave face, long jaw; as gray and dusty as the old trunk. The hellis rose up, over fields of weeds and bushes. Below them, behind a hillock, three aqua rovers stood dug in and camouflaged. They mounted huge ray guns: Remingtons. The hellis passed them by.

"The new Remingtons look more like search lights than ray guns," said Private Henley.

"They've phased out the cumbersome Wilsey. Do most everything better. They keep a few Wilseys at stress points for close in concentration capability," said the sergeant. He looked back. Private Culpepper swayed back and forth on his trunk.

They flew over a large camouflage netted area under which

appeared to be an old shock artillery car beside a generator truck and a crane. In the gray twilight it was hard to see. They passed over fields of underbrush. Dark tree-filled slopes led down to a small river, then rose up in dark hills. The sky was dark.

"I wish I was going to roar off some place on a jet," said Private Henley.

"The breaks. Private Culpepper here says he wishes he wasn't." The sergeant looked back at Private Culpepper. Private Culpepper, a grim expression on his gray face, seemed to melt into the darkness, leaving but a pale scar.

Over a flat, bare field, the hellis settled into a dark hole, stopped. A private came up to them. The sergeant showed him his pass. The private took that, the pass from Private Culpepper, the trip form from Private Henley, wrote the information on the back of his clipboard.

"This way," said the private. They followed him through the steel tube to a day room, a soft carpeted floor, contour chairs, crescent couches, bright globe lamps in soft reds, whites, yellows, greens, and blues. "Wait in here," said the private.

Privates Henley, Culpepper and the sergeant sat on a soft crescent couch. In front of them was an oval magazine table of dark glass. The sergeant picked up an Andromeda Space magazine. Private Henley picked up a deck of cards, laid out a game of solitaire called Canfield. "I hope they serve chow," he said. He had just laid out a couple of aces from the cards in his hand when the private came back.

"The captain wants to see you," he said.

The soldiers followed the private into a steel tube; to their right, into another steel tube, into an office where a captain sat behind a large computer-top desk. The soldiers came to attention and saluted.

"Stand at ease, men," boomed the captain's voice. "Sergeant, do you know anything of why the trunk was selected for the Walters Gallery?"

"No, sir."

"Or you, Private Culpepper?"

"No, sir."

"I see. The trunk will have to be cleared, of course. Private Missik, take these soldiers to chow. Then quarter them in a reserve platoon room. That is all."

The soldiers saluted, turned about and entered the steel tube, walked left, took a tube to the left, two hundred feet. Here they entered a small chow hall. They took trays, walked through an empty line, filled them, and sat at a white round table in the center of the room.

"Not bad chow," said Private Henley.

"Chow down while you got the chance," said Private Missik.

Private Culpepper sat looking at his vegetable plate. He drank a little milk.

The white table reflected its pale light on his face.

The soldiers ate what they wanted, put their trays on the tray belt, walked out, to their right a hundred feet through the shiny steel; to their right, into another steel tube one hundred and fifty feet. Somewhere they heard a bugle call. They entered into an eight bed platoon room.

"Here you are," said Private Missik. He left them.

The sergeant walked to the rear, into the latrine, taking advantage of the shiny new latrine tools, he brushed his teeth, took off his clothes, then scraped the growth of whiskers from his craggy face; he got under the shower and stood letting the warm water wash over his back, the steam rise up around his feet. Private Henley came and stood under another shower. The sergeant reached up and turned off the water knob, went to a clothes chest and selected new underwear, then into the dorm. He took the bunk next to Private Culpepper. The private was already in bed. His face looked bluish, folded in among the pale sheets.

"You feeling alright," the sergeant called over to him.

"None too good," said Private Culpepper. He lay gazing at the ceiling.

"Too long up front, I guess," said the sergeant.

"Yeah," said Private Culpepper. "Up front, it does something to you."

"Yes," said the sergeant. "It gets to you." Somewhere a bugle called. "It gets to you." The light dimmed to a gray blue. "Yes, it does. It gets to you." He looked over at Private Culpepper. The private seemed to be fading into the mist; to be, almost, not there.

The bugle blew for chow. The light in the room was golden. The sergeant dressed in a uniform from the uniform chest, walked down to the chow hall. He heard the echo of footsteps behind him, so waited up. Private Henley caught up with him; then, Private Culpepper slouching after. Together they walked through the steel tube to the chow hall. The sergeant took hot cakes, two eggs, three links of sausage, coffee and orange juice. Private Henley helped himself to hot cakes and coffee. Private Culpepper hesitated, took an egg, took orange juice. At the same table as for supper, the sergeant ate his breakfast. Private Culpepper held his glass this way, that way. He drank a little juice.

The men put up their trays, walked into the steel tube, back to the dorm. The sergeant made up his bunk. He noticed the privates following his example.

The door opened. "Men," said a husky voice of a skinny, dark-haired officer.

"Attention," said the sergeant.

"Men," repeated the officer, "I'm Lieutenant Gavombu. Fall out for exercises."

"Lieutenant, I and Private Culpepper here are on a week's special pass, sir."

"Right, Sergeant. You, private," he said to Private Henley, "fall out."

Private Henley left the dorm.

"Carry on, Sergeant," said the officer as he walked out.

By each bunk was a small table on which was a stack of letter paper, stacks of envelopes, and pens. The paper, envelopes, even the pens, had the golden Armed Forces eagle stamped on them. Sergeant Beckwith took a piece of paper, a pen, and began a letter. Private Culpepper lay on his back on his bunk. The sergeant looked over where Culpepper lay, gray and still, hardly moving at all.

"Culpepper, you do beat all Hell," said the sergeant. He looked back down at his letter, continued writing. He found himself writing the events of yesterday. He read it. "Never get through the censor," he said and doubled the papers up, threw them into a trash can.

Private Henley came in. "Whew," he said. "One two, one two." He took off his clothes and walked to the latrine.

Sergeant Beckwith took another sheet of paper. He heard the shower running and running as he wrote.

Somewhere a bugle called chow. Henley came out, dressed quickly while the sergeant got up, straightened himself out; his tie, his pants. "Come on, Private Culpepper," he called. He and Henley left and went up the tube, followed by Private Culpepper.

The soldiers entered the chow hall, put pressed meatloaf, beans and fruit compote on their trays, then sat at the table which they had claimed for theirs. Two more soldiers came in, sat at a table between them and the food counter. The sergeant and Private Henley ate their chow. Private Culpepper sat and watched. The sergeant put his fork down.

"Private Culpepper," he said in a loud voice, "It would do my heart good to see you take a good forkful of something." Private Culpepper took a forkful of fruit, put it in his mouth.

"That wasn't so bad," said the sergeant.

Private Culpepper slowly took fork after fork of fruit compote while the sergeant watched. He put his fork down.

The three of them got up and left the chow hall. "Good for you," said the sergeant to Private Culpepper. "Make your bowels move." They walked up the hall. "Make your bowels move," he said again.

They walked back up the tube, entered their dorm. Private Culpepper stretched out full length on his bed. Private Henley and the sergeant sat on their beds and the sergeant got himself a sheet of paper, put it in front of him. He looked up at Private Culpepper.

"Friend Culpepper," he said in his loud voice. "If I were you, if we are still here tomorrow; when the lieutenant comes in and says exercise, I would say, Lieutenant, I realize I'm on pass, but may I have the pleasure of your company. I would beg him to let me do some of those one two one two's. You bet I would. I think that's what I will do. Too much sitting around ain't good for a man. You weren't hit, were you, man?" The sergeant looked and seemed to see a dark spot on the private's shirt front. "But that's ridiculous," he said to Private Henley. "If he was hit bad, he couldn't be here." He looked again and didn't see it. "Besides, the fellow's changed his shirt since yesterday surely."

"What?" said Private Henley.

"Nothin' ," said the sergeant. "Just talking to myself."

He sat and looked at Private Culpepper. "I just say we all should try some of those exercises tomorrow. I'm all for 'em."

"You can have my share," said Private Henley. The sergeant bent over his paper.

"I wonder, can we check out their day room?" said Private Henley.

"I should think so. Yeah, go right ahead. They'll sure find you if they need you," said the sergeant. He concentrated on his letter. Private Henley got up and went out.

The sergeant tried to think. "Friend Culpepper," he said. "I'm trying to think what I can say interesting about the weather, the trenches, and all I can think of is jumping about just like that with that projector or whatever it was, and I know I can't even hint about that." He looked up. Private Culpepper lay stretched out on his bunk gazing up at the ceiling. "You beat all Hell, Private Culpepper," said the sergeant. He puzzled over his letter. "Maybe I'll draw a picture of one flying and let them censor that." He smiled, started drawing a crazy cartoon of himself. He smiled at the cartoon. He started to draw Private Culpepper in the trench. He started to draw. "You know, there's something fishy about that." He crossed out the picture. "Looks too spooky," he said, and put his picture aside, started writing again. He stopped, looked up. "Private Culpepper, when I get to Baltimore, if I get to Baltimore, I'm going to find the two prettiest girls in town and dance to some smooth sounds and pat their sweet tails, and squeeze them titties. Got a girl back home?"

"Don't know," said the private.

"That so? When we get to Baltimore, I'll find three; give you one of mine. But God Damn, Private Culpepper, do some exercises tomorrow, huh." The sergeant looked down and continued his letter. He got an envelope, addressed it, put his letter and picture in, got another piece of paper, started writing, stopped and thought, wrote some more.

Private Henley came in, followed by a short, dark-haired, hairy private and one who was somewhat fat, red haired, red faced.

"Well, I'm getting to be a real expert on funny books," said Private Henley. "The day room's loaded with them. Sergeant, this is Private Kilooly, the day room orderly, and here, Private Listmorack, a night mechanic. We want to know, do you want to play slip?"

"Thanks for asking. Not now. Can't you play three-hand slip?"

"Yeah, but it's not as fun. O.K. Come down if you get tired of letters." The privates went out. The sergeant wrote on his paper. He sat and thought, wrote some more.

There was a bugle call. "Chow. Come, Private Culpepper, you've got to eat if you're going to do any good in Baltimore."

The two of them got up, walked out the dorm. They walked up the tube up to the chow hall. They passed through the chow line behind the two soldiers who had eaten lunch at the table next to theirs. The sergeant and Private Culpepper took trays back to the center table. They ate. Private Henley and his two friends came through the line, came back and joined them. They ate their food.

"How was your game?" asked the sergeant.

"We didn't play. We just sat around and read funny books," said Private Henley. Kilooly.

"Sergeant, we've been curious to know about your curious trunk," said Private Kilooly.

"Don't be curious," said Private Culpepper.

"Nothing special. Nothing secret. Just some art for the Walters Gallery," said the sergeant.

"But to capture it," said Kilooly, "Sounds romantic. Where did you ever find it? You must have pulled a recon patrol out from under our cover shield. Was it under their shield, by chance? It makes my blood curdle to think of all the traps and hazards out there. And mines. And detectors. To say nothing of accidental rays and explosions and force waves. I can't guess what all your patrols are for. Trade secret, I suppose.

But if I had come across some old non-secret, non-special, non-military strategic art, I just would have left it there. You must have saved a masterpiece that will make you famous. Did you just casually walk across no-man's land carrying that great trunk?

"I think Private Culpepper's right after all," said the sergeant. "We found it kicking around in a ditch. We didn't do anything more daring than pick it up and bring it back. War is a balance of machines, detector against detector. It isn't a game for heroes."

"Gee," said Private Listmorack. "Golly."

"Yeah, there are some odd things about getting that trunk, come to think of it," said Private Henley.

"Tactical patrols are military secret, of course," said the sergeant. He finished eating. "You gentlemen excuse me, please," he said. He got up and left the chow hall, followed by Private Culpepper.

"If I'm not there, I can't talk too much," said the sergeant.

"If I'm gone I can't listen too much," said Private Culpepper.

The two walked back down the steel tube, into the dorm. The sergeant sat down, started writing. The private lay on his bed. The sergeant wrote some more, addressed an envelope, and put his letter in, took off his clothes and went to bed.

Sergeant Beckwith woke. The light in the room was golden. The bugle blew the chow call. "Up and at 'em, men," he said. "Let's go to chow." He got up, put on his clothes, walked around the room while the others rose and struggled into their clothes.

"Come on, Private Henley, you're slow as our friend Culpepper this morning. How are you going to do those old one-two one-twos if you don't get some snap." They walked out the dorm, up to the tube.

The men entered the chow hall, filled up their trays, carried them out to their table.

"Private Henley, in talking of day to day events, you never know who might be a security check agent. It might be a smart talking fellow who knows a lot. It might be a fellow who says 'gee whiz' and 'golly' and little else," said Sergeant Beckwith.

"Yeah, that's so, Sergeant," said Private Henley.

The sergeant ate his stew, his pudding, drank his coffee. He got up from the table and the other men with him. They went out of the chow hall, up the steel tube. The wavery light shining off the walls flickered on them as they walked. Their shoes echoed on the hard floor. The sergeant watched their reflections on the walls flicker and waver. "Some reflections," he said. The tall, pale reflection of Private Culpepper faded in and out; sometimes there, sometimes merged into patches of shiny light. Up the tube they walked, to the dorm. They entered. The sergeant walked back to the latrine. He heard another person enter the dorm.

"Captain Bwanahab wants to see you soldiers," said Private Missik. "Where's the sergeant?"

"Be out in a minute," called Sergeant Beckwith.

"The sergeant came into the dorm, and the four of them stepped into the bright tunnel, walked down, around, up to the office of the captain. They entered, saluted.

"At ease," spoke the heavy voice of the captain. "The, ah, trunk has been inspected. Odd, but there's little risk of contamination or anything dangerous coming from it. We don't know what use it could have, but it seems those scientific birds from Lamar have found something useful about it. You may take it to the Walters. Private Missik, there is a jet for Baltimore at zero seven zero this afternoon. See that those two there are one it with their trunk. And, Private Henley, return immediately to your outfit. That is all."

The soldiers saluted and left the office. Private Missik told Private Henley, "Private, I'll take you to your hellis. It's been cleared for exit."

"You all have a good trip," said Private Henley. Here the soldiers parted ways; the two going one way, the other two going the other.

The sergeant and Private Culpepper walked up the tube to their dorm, went in. The sergeant took off his clothes and laid them on his bed. He looked up to see Private Culpepper on the next bed

126

over, stretched out, staring at the ceiling. The sergeant went into the latrine, brushed his teeth, shaved, got under the warm shower. The shower water ran on him and warmed him. He turned it off, went to the clothes chest, put on new underwear, a new shirt, new pants, new jacket. He went back into the dorm, fixed his tie, got his letters together and put them in his pocket, left the dorm and went up the tube, walked through the shiny walls to the day room. The sergeant sat on a contoured chair, picked up a nomardik magazine off the table. He leafed through it, looking at the diagrams of the nomardik force fields. The bugle's chow call interrupted his studies. "Chow time," he said.

Sergeant Beckwith put up the magazine and got up, walked back out into the tube. He walked through the steel walls of flickering reflections to the dorm. He looked in, called, "Come on, Private Culpepper. Chow."

The private got up. He and the sergeant walked together through the bright walls of the tube. They got to the chow hall, entered, got trays, followed Private Missik and two other soldiers through the food line. The soldiers in front of them went to a table in the back of the room. The sergeant took his usual place at the center table, and Private Culpepper sat across from him. The private sat and watched the sergeant, nibbled on a piece of bread, sat and watched some more. Sergeant Beckwith sipped his coffee.

Private Missik came up to the sergeant's table. "Sergeant," he said, "It's time for you and the private here to board your jet."

"Lead the way," said Sergeant Beckwith. The three of them walked out of the chow hall, down the tube. They turned right, walked down another tube. They came to a door. They passed through the door, which was two doors; the second door, the door of the jet.

"The trunk is on board, and here are the travel papers," Private Missik said as he handed Sergeant Beckwith the papers. The private left. The door slid shut, and the jet slid out of the dock into the bright blue day. Beyond the transparent sidings, the sergeant could see blue sky and fleecy white clouds. He sat down, sharing a seat with Private Culpepper. In front of him, two officers with dark grayish hair sat rattling papers, which they had on their laps on the top of their briefcases. Twenty other officers were in seats in front of these. No one spoke. The jet sped through the blue.

The jet descended, slowed, passed into a dark tunnel, stopped. Everyone filed off the jet onto a white platform. There was a glass ceiling way above them. The floor was like a white pool of water at the bottom of a white-sided well. The platform started rising, stopped, panels slid back. Everyone stepped off the platform, into a lobby, onto a thick green carpet, walked around the circles of soft blue easy chairs, and soft beige easy chairs. A private was in the lobby looking at papers and directing the travelers to one door or another. The private came over and checked the sergeant's papers.

"Third door from the right," he said.

The sergeant and Private Culpepper walked through the lobby and out the door. Parked in the drive, there was a long, shiny brown limousine, the old dusty trunk in the back of it. The private and the sergeant got into the vehicle behind the drive's seat. The limousine started and drove down the driveway.

The driveway rose up, circled around shiny buildings of pale glass, led into a white road flanked with evergreens. They sped along the empty road toward the tall buildings of a city. Then the tall white, blue, tan, and gray buildings were on either side of them. They turned off the white road, drove slowly down an old road. Crowds of people got out of the road, out of their way. The low buildings on either side were of a great variety of shapes, indicating a span of a great many ages; some of the buildings being of a great antiquity. The limousine turned down a street to the left. Even greater crowds of people got out of the street, out of their way. The buildings on this street, ancient brick, gray or brown stone, were generally older than those on the street from which they turned. People crowded on to sidewalks to let them pass. "No sign of a shortage of people here," said the sergeant.

The limousine pulled up in front of a square, gray stone building. Over a long, wide flight of white stone steps were large metal doors. Above the doors were letters cut in the stone. They read, "WALTERS GALLERY OF ART". Sergeant Beckwith and Private Culpepper dismounted, climbed the steps and entered through a door to the side of the great center doors.

"We are here to see Dr. Rhodes," the sergeant told the uniformed man who was standing near the door.

"The office at the top of the stairs on your left," said the man in uniform.

The soldiers walked up the stairs under a row of dark, dusty paintings, and the sergeant knocked at the door at the top.

A grey-bearded man opened the door. "Ah, the soldiers of the mysterious trunk, no doubt. The great puzzle. I'm Dr. Rhodes. The gentlemen at Lamar were contacted and claimed no knowledge of any trunk, but were interested. They suggested that it might be connected with some special project of Major Halstead's. The Major, no doubt, will tell us all about what's in the trunk when we locate him."

"Sir," said Sergeant Beckwith, "I don't think the major knows what's in the trunk. He just saw that the label on the outside said 'Art' so he directed it here."

"The.information I got about it was that it contained some strange matter of an undetermined nature. At first, the old dusty trunk being sent to the Walters with nothing in it remotely resembling art made them suspicious of a hoax. But with the reputation Lamar has, they figured it might have to do with some odd experiments of the major's which he didn't want other scientists to meddle into, so thought they better get it clearance. But the security check team ran into some strange problems with the contents. First, the amount of matter in it seemed to fluctuate. Second, they ran into problems in determining what some of the matter was. I mean the checks were contra dictory; elements which would not normally be gaseous lingering in the trunk in a gaseous state. With these problems, the military got in touch with Lamar immediately. Lamar will send a team of scientists to investigate. What's the matter with your friend? Is he ill?"

The sergeant looked at Private Culpepper, who was to his left. The private looked ill, his skin bluish-gray and his eyes almost trance-like.

"I don't think he feels well," said the sergeant. "He's been off his feed."

"I hope you're soon feeling better, Private," said Dr. Rhodes. "And another thing. You men are to be guests of Lamar's at the Histafu House. They would like to have you available in case they want to question you. We are all sure you will want to cooperate.

"Yes, sir," said the sergeant.

"Well, gentlemen. Enjoy the Histafu House." "Thank you, sir," said the sergeant.

The soldiers went down the stairs, out of the Walters, got into their waiting limousine. The sergeant noticed that the box was gone.

The vehicle drove them back up the crowded street. Four blocks up, they turned left. This was also a crowded street. The crowds got out of their way. The crowds got sparse as they drove on, the buildings became old, ramshackle warehouses and vacant buildings, some fallen in ruins. There were a couple of dingy stores and a flop house type of building which the paintless sign on its front called Harwood Hotel. There were bums in front, three unshaven men in baggy, dirty suits. The limousine stopped because a dark-skinned woman in run-down shoes was crossing the street in her old, slow way. Private Culpepper got out, stumbled down the old, cracked sidewalk, up into the hotel.

"I'll be a son of a bitch," said the sergeant. The limousine drove on.

The limousine turned right, past stone houses with dirty children in front of them; past bright glass houses, all with white glass steps in front of them The driver took a left. Here was a park of green grass and white arched bridges. The park ended in a grove of weeping willows. Beyond these, twisting glass towers. The driver pulled up front and stopped. The sergeant got out.

Sergeant Beckwith walked a few yards up a glass sidewalk. The sidewalk dipped and became a bright white tunnel filled with statues and waterfalls along its walls. The tunnel opened out to a room like a small park. There were glass arches which climbed among trees, around fountains, around pools of water. One side of the room was a rocky cliff over which water flowed in numerous little falls.

A gentleman in a gray suit was seated on a white glass bench. He got up, came over. The light made his gray hair seem silvery. It was a soft lavender light.

"Good evening. You are Sergeant Beckwith, I presume? I'm Mr. Barfog. We're glad to have you. If you like, I'll show you to your room. Then you may rest, wander about, or call on me, and I will keep you company. As you may know, we use the latel service which can put you within an easy walk of any place in town."

As the gentleman spoke, the floor on which they stood was rising. Many of the arches and trees were way below them. They stepped into a room.

"The comforts of home," the gentleman was saying". He pointed to the large, abstract bed; the mirrored dressing cabinet covered with crystal toilet articles; the huge, pool-like bath; the telecomo stand.

"If there is any way we can be of help, please call on us. Use our dining room at your convenience. Our telecomo will give you any directions which you need. I'll see you later."

Sergeant Beckwith found himself alone. His first thought was that his room had no privacy, but he looked at the large open area behind him, and he discovered barriers of light. There seemed a great expanse of space, but he could not see past the confines of what must be called his room. He found his barrier control knob on the telecomo, the barrier keyed so that only he could move through it to get in and out. Secure now in his privacy, he took off his clothes, got into his pool. He found a fountain control knob which gave a splendid shower effect. He set the fountain on a mist and played in his pool.

Sergeant Beckwith, floating in the water, decided he was hungry. He got out of the pool, dried off, dressed in a shiny robe and comfortable slippers, went to his telecomo and contacted Food Service.

"Hello, Sergeant. Would you like to join us in our dining room? It isn't a large crowd, but we are enjoying ourselves," said the lady in the telecomo.

"I think tomorrow. I'm a bit tired today. I'll join you tomorrow, I think. Could I please have something sent up?"

"You certainly may. What would you like? Would you like me to describe some of my favorites?"

"I would like a good German dinner, whatever the chef likes to cook. But no hurry. An hour to an hour and a half would be fine."

"Splendid. Our German food is a good choice, and our cook will be pleased to have a free hand on it. We'll get started on it."" The picture faded.

The sergeant went to his control panel and played with the knobs of his light barriers. The barrier faded over his outside walls revealing translucent and transparent glass arches covered with arabesques. Outside, there were a number of glass arches leading from and twisting around the building. The sergeant walked out on his balcony. At one end, it curved up and out into a great arch. The other end of the balcony sunk and twisted around the building. The sun had just set, and the sky was bathed in pink light. On all sides rose the spires and towers of the city. The sergeant went back in and readjusted his light barriers, then lay on the comfortable bed.

A gentleman entered with a silver tray. The light glittered on the silver, shone on the bald head of the gentleman as he arranged a black, slender-legged table, set the tray on it, set a dark chair in front of it. He went out.

The sergeant got off the bed and sat at the table, ate all the German food set there. The gentleman returned in his dark suit, took the tray away. The sergeant reset his light barrier, lay on his bed and sleep came to him as-he lay there.

The sergeant woke. The sunlight shone through the translucent light barriers.

The sergeant went to his telecomo. "Good morning. Breakfast?" said the lady. "Yes, please. Pancakes and coffee."

"Coming right up," said the telecomo.

The sergeant went over and adjusted his light harriers. He turned a knob and the latrine appeared. The sergeant used the toiled, a glass and crystal bowl; washed at a white and silver basin, brushed his teeth and shaved, readjusted the barrier. The gentleman in the dark suit entered, put the silver tray on the dark table. The sergeant sat and ate his pancakes. The gentleman came back in and took the silver tray away.

Sergeant Beckwith went over and played with the light screen knobs. Screens shifted in and out in different colors. A floor screen dissolved. There was a slender woman in a bathrobe, playing with her knobs. She smiled up at him. He smiled back. Slowly, the misty light reformed the screen. Beyond the latrine, a screen dissolved.

Here were uniforms, new sergeant's uniforms, all with his brigade insignia. They were new and of the finest materials. There they were: an A dress uniform with all his medals on the coat (he had never worn an A uniform); the B uniform, his normal dress uniform; the C battle dress with the battle jacket and knickers; the D work dress with the work shirt and field jacket; the E field dress, which served as a sport uniform, as a class and duty uniform, even at times, as battle dress; the F casual uniform and the G work uniform.

"Culpepper should see these," he said. He undressed, jumped in the bath, washed, got out, dressed in clean shirt and underclothes, put on the C uniform, left his room for the elevation floor and descended to the patio.

The gentleman in gray was seated by the pool under some palm trees. He looked up.

"Good morning. You look as if a good night's rest agreed with you."

"It did. I feel splendid. By the way, there was a friend of mine supposed to be with me. Do you think it would be alright if I brought him over?"

"A Private Culpepper? Sure. I'm sorry I I haven't had the pleasure of meeting him sooner."

"You hadn't mentioned him. I wasn't sure you were aware of him."

"I was. You know, we attempt to supply the most possible comfort, the finest in aesthetic pleasures and the greatest amount of courtesy which our civilization has developed. Courtesy and manners are mostly kindness, consideration and making people comfortable. Yet, some people are uncomfortable here, largely because the highest degrees of civilization is unfamiliar to them. Sometimes, they don't give us a try because they are afraid of being made to feel out of place. These are mistaken notions. We who have material things attempt to never lord it over anyone who has few of them. We try to never make manners a shield for hypocrisy and insincerity or a sacred code by which we bar our fellow man. Our fellow man need not be afraid of what I call our virtues. Of course, there are people who have pleasures which we here don't find pleasurable. For instance, we miss the excitement of barroom brawls because we prefer not to relate to our fellow man in that way. We have no call girls for the same reason.

For much the same reason, we accept no tips. We prefer to be generous and gentle because we like people. I think those who enjoy being inconsiderate of others would be happier in some place else. If your friend likes people and was, perhaps, skeptical of all our comfort and good manners, I would like a chance to teach him that we have some thing to offer."

"I don't think my friend had any of those reasons for not coming. I think he is ill and afraid he'll be a drag on my good times."

"Is he then in an infirmary?"

"No. He went to the Harwood Hotel."

"Harwood. I've never heard of it. That could be a plus, because I seldom hear good things about hotels. I think the most cold-blooded and rascally and inhuman are those which charge the most. Some holes in the wall which charge a copper penny are the most human. Come to think of it, when I was a little child there was a Harwood Hotel. It was once considered elegant and even in my time retained some of its antique charm. I don't suppose that old building could be still standing. Well, if you find your friend, tell him he's invited."

"Thank you, sir. I'm going over there now. Say, how do you use the latel service you mentioned?"

"Those floor controls by your hand will put you at tube level. Select a latel and dial your address."

"I don't know the address. Would telecomo have it?"

Mr. Barfog produced a small telecomo from under the seat. "Hello. May I ask what is the location of the Harwood Hotel? Thanks so much." He wrote on a small pad, gave the slip to the sergeant. "And take this list with you, too."

"Thank you, Mr. Barfog."

"Glad to help. It's my pleasure."

Sergeant Beckwith turned the knob. The floor sank. Around the platform, hovering in the air, were small ships, similar in size and shape to a canoe. A few were larger. He climbed into a small one, set the dials according to his slip of paper. The latel floated under a white arch, down a white tunnel. As the latel floated, he looked at the printed list Mr. Barfog had given him. It was a list of clubs, restaurants, and entertainment places. The latel came to a dock and stopped. He got out, climbed a curving gray stone stairway. He came up on a sidewalk in front of some houses of green stone. Walking down the street, he came to the street where the old buildings were and not too far from the Harwood. The few people in the street here seemed old and poor. These he passed and entered the hotel through a little hall into a lobby of worn furniture, cracked plaster, and spider webs. At a kitchen type table, crudely made and nearly paintless, two old men sat at checkers. In an iron cage was a white-haired man wearing horn rimmed spectacles.

"I'm here to visit Private Culpepper." Announced the sergeant. "Room 17," said the elderly clerk.

"Do you know, is he in?"

"All I know, he paid his rent and went up. No one's seen him since. I was getting ready to knock on his door and inquire as to his health. Do let us know if he isn't well. We have a doctor comes here when we need him, and he doesn't charge us 'cause most of the folks who stay here, they couldn't pay."

"Thank you. I will." The sergeant walked up the narrow old stairway, three flights. There was Room 17. He knocked. No answer. He called, "May I come in?"

"Yeah," came the sound like an echo. Sergeant Beckwith entered. There was Private Culpepper sitting in a straight-backed wooden kitchen chair gazing somewhat out the window, but not seeming to be really looking at anything. He was sitting sort of sideways to the window.

"I thought you were going clubbing with me," said Sergeant Beckwith. The private sat and watched the clouds go by.

"Well, god damn, you can't sit in this chair all week." Sergeant Beckwith looked at the private's grayish face. Shadows from somewhere seemed to fall across it, and in their dark hollows, the eyes reminded the sergeant of those of a blind man.

"And the clerk at the desk says you haven't been out to eat nothing. We can't have that. A soldier has to eat. Look man, I brought with me a list of the best eating places in Baltimore. I want you to go with me to one of them. You choose any you like, eat to your heart's content. The treats on me." The sergeant opened the list, "Abercrombies's, Avalon, Ace, Baker's, Billicut's, Binsinoti, Bundy's Tavern, CuCu Clock, Casement's, Chill's Will's, Cellar Dwellers, Dumbarton, Dorsey's Wharf, Duffy & Cotton, East of Suez, Eggbert's, Fisherman's, Fishbein's Delicatessen, Flytell's, Camden Station, Driftwood House, Diamond Jim's, Arts & Crafts, Actors' Lodge, Burl Ives' Coffee House, Frank House Hall, Flying Flag Bar, Gitting's, Halta, Frenzied Fool, Frisky Pup, Gormagong, Geek The Greek, Golden Dragon, Gray Gable, Hurly Bus, Idle Boy, Just For Kicks, Killikoola's Pow Wow, Little John's, Love Birds, Lowenfeld's, Miller Brothers, Monocacy, Moon Madness, Messerschmidt's, North City, Nollsnutter's, Normandy Fields, Old Dutch, Olney Inn, Peter Quirk's, Pillouawatt, Pitt Circus, Peabody Bookshop - Peabody Bookshop. Well, that's the first one you didn't shake your head at. I don't know whether you just got tired of shaking your head, but that's where we're going, so up and at 'em."

Private Culpepper stood up. Together they walked out and down the stairs. The old man in the cage smiled at them as they went out. They walked up to the latel entrance, walked down the steps to the docks, got in a latel, and the sergeant set the dials according to the address on his list. The latel floated down the tunnel. The private's features seemed to mingle with the shadows of the arches and the reflections on the walls. They rode in silence. The latel docked. The soldiers.got out. Private Culpepper followed the sergeant up the narrow, dark stairway, on to the street. This was an old street, but there seemed to be numbers of people walking along or shopping in the small and ancient brick and stone stores. They came to what seemed a most ancient building. The sign over the door said "Peabody Bookshop". They went in. There was a short, gray-haired man in a baggy suit standing by, of all things, a cash register. The cash register was about three feet tall and somewhat ornate. It was a store filled with shelves on shelves of old, faded, dusty books.

"And how are you young gentlemen today?"

"We're still kicking," said the sergeant. "Say, this is a bookstore."

"And a rare bird it is in today's world, what with cidibells, telereels, flickascopes, arniffs, and all. Few people read books nowadays. And a shame it is. It's much more exciting to read, do your own picture painting from the bare suggestiveness of the author, than to have all

136

your work done for you by all those video machines. But books are a thing of the past. They still make a few. But a shop that makes books is about as rare as a shop that sells 'em. A few magazines are printed; mostly for the armed forces, I think."

The short man walked to a shelf of dusty books. "Now this is a book, was printed last year. It's sort of like poetry. Modem times contribution to literature. But if it's stories you want, here's an old book by Belfalloran. A real fire he has. Or that one by Cosmalo. That one is the poetry of Munt Blazingame. That one, a novel by Eli Shistis. And this old dusty book is some of the prettiest story-telling you'll find. It's by Cloyden Dwevelavan. You can knock the dust off the shelves and look through them to your heart's content."

Sergeant Beckwith picked up the book by Dwevelavan out of the shelf, leafed through it. "Is this the price?

"Yes, it is."

"Then here is a bill that will cover it and take out for a book for my friend too." "I've read nary a book," said the private.

"Then here is an old replica of a very early book from close to the days when printing was new. The old book itself would be a collector's item, but this replica can be purchased, and the sergeant here still have a little change corning back. It's called Just So Stories. It will be a good first book."

"That's fine," said the sergeant. "But where is the Peabody Bookshop Restau rant? We saw it on a list of restaurants."

"I didn't know there was such a list. But we serve meals here."

The short man walked over to a bookcase on the back wall, pulled it out a little. Behind it was a low tunnel which led to a dimly lit room. The soldiers took their books and squeezed into the passage, down into the room. Three men were seated on wooden chairs at the only table in the room, a long heavy wooden table, glasses of dark liquid in front of them.

"Hello there. Won't you come and join us?" they called.

The soldiers went and sat next to one of the men and facing the other two. A bell rang in a tall mechanism which stood on the floor and reached to a head taller than the height of the average man.

"What is that?" said the sergeant.

"It's called a grandfather clock," said the man who sat next to him. "It rang eleven, which is the number this hour of the day would have been called when that thing was made. It is ancient, as is that desk beside it. In fact, the desk is likely older than the clock."

The desk had, above the writing surface, shelves of books behind glass doors. "More books," said the sergeant.

"Other rare items in this modem world," said the man on the other side of the table and nearest the fireplace, an old brick fireplace on the opposite wall to the one from which they had entered.

The sergeant looked behind him at the ornate sideboard covered with old chinaware cruets, decanters, and other antique dining room items.

"That sideboard," said the man next to the sergeant, "dates back to about the same period as the clock. Some of the things on it are older. Then, on the mantle over the fireplace, the steins next to the deer's skull are ancient. That vase at the end of the mantle is very old. The carvings, some are old, some are not so old. About the only modem thing in the room is the picture over the mantle."

The room was dark and shadowy, the only light coming in wavy patterns from the wavy glass in the small window between the desk and the wall with the fireplace.

Wavy shadows of something flitted across the skull in the center of the mantle. "What is that to the left of the skull?" asked the sergeant.

"That is called a Chinese water pipe," said the man next to him. "Let me introduce myself. I'm Sport Sodastrom, the man on my left there is Carbon Blankenship, and that is Emil Vlabudu."

Blankenship got out a pipe, reached over to the hearth and banged it, filled it with fresh herbs, lit it. "This place is fun at night when they have folk singers. They light it with candles. Then, in cool weather, they have a fire."

"Sport is a musician himself. He plays a violin," said Blankenship.

"But only when I'm not repairing cars. But Carbon actually sells paintings for a living. He painted those ships or whatever they are over the mantle. And Emil coaches kids' mathematics, plays chess in

138

his spare time."

A tall, bony woman came in. "Tell Mrs. Byrd what you want to eat, but talk loud because she doesn't hear too well," said Carbon.

"Mrs. Byrd," said the sergeant. "I'd like to start with something to drink, please."

"Mulled cider, mulled wine, coffee, tea?"

"Mulled cider for me. What for you, friend Culpepper?" The private nodded. "Make it two," said the sergeant.

Mrs. Byrd left.

"I'm Howard Beckwith and this here is Wallace Culpepper."

"How did you find us here, Sergeant," asked Sport.

"I have this little old list they gave me at my hotel." He got the list out of the book he was carrying, handed it to Sport.

"Why, this is the Histafu. They don't even have a desk clerk at the Histafu. You almost have to be invited, like a private party. I would love to stay there, if I could afford it."

"I think you save up, like you would for a vacation," said the sergeant.

Mrs. Byrd brought in two mulled ciders. The sergeant sipped his. "This is really good."

"It should be," said Vlabudu, "About everything they serve here is produced by backwoods Maryland farms, sort of like bootleg. The cheese is unpasturized, the cider is fermented, the beer is without preservatives, the ham is sugar cured, and the vegetables are full-flavored, non-commercial types. Real old-fashioned varieties."

The men sipped their drinks. Blankenship smoked his pipe. The clock sounded a single loud bong. Shadows from things passing the window swept the room, dimming the light in the room suddenly.

"The shadows sure look strange crossing the private's face," said Sodastrom. "From an artist's point of view, I mean. Like, it would make a strange painting. It's just that the shadow is so dark on him, on the back wall, it looks continuous. Strange things, shadows."

The sergeant looked over at Private Culpepper. The private sat lost in thought. "Bet he didn't even hear your comment about him and shadow. It's maybe concave people attract shadow," said the sergeant.

"Bovatikou wrote about concave people, or what he called bent in people. He said they suck in mirth," said Vlabudu. He sipped his drink. The clock ticked. Some where outside, a dog howled. Another dog barked somewhere far away.

"Our city animal life," said Sport.

The rear door slid open, and an elderly man came down to the table. His clothes were somewhat threadbare, and his hair hung over his ears.

Sport said, "Here is Mr. Nagastacrel. He's retired. A shoe salesman. Hello, Mr. Nagastacrel. These are our friends Sergeant Beckwith and Private Culpepper," Mrs. Byrd came out. Mr. Nagastacrel said, "Stout and apple pie."

Sport said, "That's four stout."

The sergeant said, "Stout, ham sandwich and apple pie for me and the private, here."

"Armed Forces men," said Mr. Nagastacrel. "The Armed Forces must be an exciting place to be these days. Yes sir, two struggling armies."

"It can be," said the sergeant.

"Yes sir, from time to time they thought war was going to be obsolete. With one big bang, one side was going to win. Then they discovered distance detonators, and nations couldn't make anything explosive any more. Then they had the germ bombs.

Then they got immunity pills. And then they still had wars. Yes sir, there was the use of Brazil and the age of General Gaustez. Then there was old Lumbust and his army. Yes, sir. Never be another general like Fino Lumbust. And all the ways they'd invented for killing people. You could make a year of telly specials and not show them all," said Mr. Nagastacrel.

"I'd rather be a private that had done one heroic thing, than a general that had invented the greatest bomb on earth," said Sodastrom.

Carbon puffed on his pipe. "Where are you staying, Private Culpepper?"

"The Harwood."

"That's one I don't know," said Sport. "Me, neither," Carbon said.

Mr. Nagastacrel told them, "No, you all wouldn't have heard of that. 'Cause you aren't old folks. Old folks hear of places like that, 'cause they have different needs. Your nice swanky new places; The Acom, The Armbuster: they aren't right for old folks. First, being wards of the state, they are trying to pinch pennies so they don't starve on that penny dole. Second, they don't find this new-fangled furniture restful.

Third, for them the young people move too fast and are too loud. Folks don't like to be bumped into; nor to have young folks tapping their feet, showing impatience with the slowness which comes with age. Then, lots of crooks hang around those rich hotels, making them unsafe for old folks. Even if they were safe and reasonably priced, the cold, impersonal help always hollering tip or additional charge would run old folks away. In an old folks hotel, nobody bothers the customers, and the gentleman behind the desk is usually considerate. Chances are, he's getting on toward old himself. Now and again, bums and winos rent rooms at these hotels; particularly at the cheaper, sleazier ones. But they really don't bother anybody. Sometimes those cheap old hotels can seem sort of like home. The people there usually have one thing in common: they're old. Oh, now and again some soldier, looking for drinks or excitement, down the lower end of town finds these old hotels as being the most convenient shelter for passing off their hangover. And soldiers, if they come in rowdy from the tavern, the sight of a couple of old grandmothers in a lobby makes them find their manners quick enough. How about you, Private? Am I right? You drinking at those all-night bars somewhere down around Fayette Street find the Harwood the next convenient place to stumble into?"

"I wam't drinking."

"Well, soldiers often sack out in places where as civilians they would never go," said Mr. Nagastacrel.

"Mrs. Byrd isn't baking the bread for those sandwiches, is she?" asked the sergeant.

"Mrs. Byrd thinks like this. You ordered close to lunch time what obviously you intended to be lunch. But it wasn't quite time for lunch, according to her figuring. She'll have your lunch in plenty of time for you to eat at 12:00," Mr. Nagastacrel said. "By that clock, I mean."

"Well, what about our drinks?" the sergeant wanted to know.

"Mrs. Byrd is never in a hurry to bring drinks, particularly to young folks who are not yet old and set in their ways. I can tell she approves of you. That would make her even slower with drinks." Mr. Nagastacrel turned and looked at the clock. "I kinda like the anticipation, waiting for my drink."

Carbon puffed on his pipe. Sport suggested, "Maybe people should take up pipe smoking as a social activity."

Mrs. Byrd came in with drinks and lunches on a dark tray, served them, collected her money, left the room. The clock bell rang twelve times. The sergeant looked up at it, said, "Now we can eat." The men smiled.

Sergeant Beckwith took a sip of stout, took a bite of the home-baked bread sandwich, old country sugar cured ham and water cress. "Good sandwich."

Mr. Nagastacrel started on his apple pie served, as it was, with a wedge of sharp cheese. The sergeant finished his sandwich, started on apple pie.

"Sergeant, you get a chance for doing much sightseeing when you're over seas?" asked Mr. Vlabudu.

"Depends on what sights you mean." The sergeant ate some pie. "I'm not much of a sight-seer, but I enjoy seein' what other countries are like." He finished his pie, sat and thought. The clock bell rang.

"Sometimes," said the sergeant. "Just the dirt and the trees in other countries look different. Then I like to go through cities, listen to people not knowing what they're sayin'."

The men sipped their drinks. Private Culpepper watched the windows.

Through the window could be seen the bottoms of things and the shadows of moving things. A small bird flitted past. The men sat over their drinks.

A man wearing tan britches and a tan shirt entered. A large, red-faced man; bald, but red hair around the sides of his head. "Afternoon, gentlemen."

"Hi, Captain. Captain, this is Sergeant Beckwith and Private Culpepper. Men, Captain Rapahonock", said Carbon.

"Hi do, Sir," said the sergeant. Carbon went on to say, "The Captain has his tug in the harbor."

"I would think jets would make shipping by water a thing of the past," the sergeant said to the captain.

"And they may some day, but in this day and age, jets are still too expensive and impractical for some areas. Take the bay area - Cambridge, Crisfield, they don't particularly want jets over there. Then, some heavy, bulky products are more easily shipped over the waves. Ships, often quite a satisfactory business." Mrs. Byrd came in.

"Mrs. Byrd, a ham and turkey, please, and a nut brown. Emil, is the govern ment as nosy as ever as to what you say in the classroom?" the captain said.

"You know they are."

"Are there any dodges that you all use? Don't give away any of your trade secrets, but are there dodges that are usually used?"

"I sponsor clubs. Then, in the club, I'm fellow member Mr. Vlabudu. But my conversational opinions about things, I'm sure, carry weight."

"What is the usual opinion, or some of the opinions, which the students express about the war?" Carbon asked.

"They think it's stupid to fight. They think the war was unnecessary and could have been avoided. My apology, Sergeant."

"I'm more interested in the Sergeant's opinion of the war and, if it's changed since his student days; if so, for what cause," said the captain.

"You may have them and welcome. I offer them without apology, for my opinions are the best I can do. The war may be everything the students say, but I still think there is some virtue in joining with your fellows and striving for a thing, even though the goal be a myth. We were called to serve the land of our fathers, so we went. The Germans are doing the same thing, and I don't put myself better or smarter than them. I'm more interested, and you should be, too, in Private Culpepper's opinion."

The clock bell rang. Mr. Nagastacrel turned and looked at the clock. "Excuse me, gentlemen." He got up.

"As far as the Germans," said Blankenship, "we can't be much smarter or dedicated than they, or we wouldn't have this fantastic stalemate. Sergeant, why Private Culpepper's over any other?"

Mrs. Byrd entered, put the sandwich and glass of nut brown in front of the captain.

"Because he's seen it from rock bottom."

"Mrs. Byrd, I think we are all ready for refills on our drinks," said Carbon. "Not me," said Mr. Nagastracrel. "I'm just waiting a second."

"With morning, the sun rises in the east and it is light. The sun sets into the west and darkness comes. What opinion could I have?" said Private Culpepper.

"It was nice to make your acquaintance, Private Culpepper, Sergeant Beckwith." Mr. Nagastracrel left.

"Sounds sibylic," said Carbon.

"My great, great, great, great-grandfather fought under General Stelfox. My great, great, great-grandfather fought on under General Ulstamoto. My great-grandfather fought under General Showenfizen. My father was a soldier under General Paulmoll. Now, here I am, doing my best for General Moojay. So right or wrong, in a way, we'll be together some place," said the sergeant.

"Quite a family history," said the captain. He drank his ale. Mrs. Byrd brought drinks in, collected money, went out.

"There is something romantic in a soldier's life, I'm sure. More than that. I should say glorious. But the soldier may himself see very little of the romance," said Mr. Vlabudu.

"You mean, the knight usually doesn't slay the dragon and have a fair maiden to carry off?" Carbon asked.

"No, I mean the knight doesn't understand and appreciate his own heroics, as much as he might."

The men drank their drinks.

"What do you all plan to do when you get out of the armed forces?" asked Carbon.

"Me, I would like to do lots of things. Sail ships with the captain. Maybe paint pictures like Blankenship. Herd cattle and sing songs 'round campfires at night. Stay at my beautiful hotel and fill my room there with music and beautiful women. Then maybe I would take them to the ocean, and we would all swim out on the waves.

Whatever I do, it's going to be fun."

"You can sail with me any time you like, Sergeant," said the captain. "And you?" Carbon asked Private Culpepper.

"I don't know," he said.

The sunlight came in the window in wavy lights and darks. It shone on the heavy glasses as one after another of the men raised a glass to his lips. The clock bell rang. The clocks works jangled inside its great body.

"Can you go back to the Histafu after you get out of the army?" Sport asked. "I mean, a millionaire could walk in there, not know who to pay his million to, so he would have to just walk out again."

"I think I could."

"The Histafu?" said the captain, "Sergeant, you must have captured a general."

"No, nothing so glamorous."

"Well, Sergeant, if you would like to tell your exploit, I would enjoy hearing it."

"It's as much Private Culpepper's exploit as mine. Even more, if it was an exploit at all."

"How about that, Private Culpepper? Would you call it an exploit?" the captain asked.

"I wouldn't know," said Private Culpepper.

"No real mystery," said Sergeant Beckwith. "We found a box and brought to Merika. It was more accident than exploit, to be truthful."

"It all sounds to me like an exploit," said the captain, "but of a mysterious nature. And, as things of a mysterious nature connected with the armed forces are usually secret; I probably had better say no more about it."

"Up front," said the sergeant, "taking a piss is top secret if the soldier tells where he pissed. It's even a problem writing letters, when your activity for every minute of the day would be classified as secret."

The men sat and drank.

Two high school aged girls entered carrying backpacks in their hands. "Hello," said the captain. "Packs and wearing slacks. Going camping?"

"No, just an easy way to bum around," said the small red-haired girl.

"Yeah. We're drop-outs," said the taller blonde. She laughed.

They sat down, the blonde next to the captain, the redhead next to the sergeant.

"I feel so romantic sitting next to a soldier," said the redhead. "I can tell you two are from overseas."

"Then," said Mr. Vladbudu, "I say, some times the knight slays the dragon and flies away with the beautiful lady."

"Only, in this case," said Carbon, "as with most cases in modem war; 'tis a strange-looking dragon which they slay."

"What kind of dragon, Sergeant?" the blonde asked.

"In short terms, war has guns and explosives and rays instead of fiery serpents, but I can't be specific. It's against the rules."

"Then we won't ask."

There was a minute of silence. "We're waiting for you to find another way to ask," said the captain. There was laughter around the table. The sergeant sipped his drink.

"How did you get your scar?" the blonde asked Private Culpepper.

"It runs from your eye all the way down your cheek."

"Training accident. Slipped during sino training."

"I thought maybe you got it fighting the enemy."

"In the armed forces," said the sergeant, "near all the fighting is done during training, unless you're in an outfit that does its fighting for recreation in drinking establishments. Against the enemy, that's just up front. In my great-grandfather's time, they used to call that going into combat. But now it's just up front. There's very little fighting up front. Either you get it or you don't. And you can get it before you even know you're up front."

The redhead asked the sergeant, "What's sino?"

"Learning how to make a weapon of your body." The men sat over their drinks.

The clock bell rang, rang again.

"Speaking of flying away," said the sergeant, "we'd better check with my hotel.

Drink up, friend Culpepper. Is there a telecomo here? I had really better call."

"Two doors down, the drug shop has one. Odd how some people never get one; can exist without what so many think is an absolute must," said Carbon.

"Come, private Culpepper, for all I know, we might be holding up the works," said the sergeant.

"Can we walk on the street with you two to the drugshop. It would be so much fun."

"Sure, come along," said the sergeant.

"Thank you. Come on, Star," said the redhead.

The four of them went up through the opening, pushed the bookcase out and went into the bookshop, through the shop and out to the street, down to the second store. The store said Destel Drugs. Inside, the store was filled with old racks of soaps and lotions. The druggist, in his white jacket, stood behind the drug counter. They went up to the counter.

"Good evening sir, I'm sergeant Beckwith, on a special assignment. May I get you to check my hotel and see if there are any special orders for me."

"Certainly sergeant. I'd be glad to run a telecall for you even if it were not something of vital importance. Here we go," he got out his telecomo, "at what hotel are you staying?"

"Histafu House."

"Histafu house?" the druggist said in surprise. "Histafu House? Gee," said the redhead

"Yes, Stit's my name. I'm calling for Sergeant Beckwith. There are? Just a second." The druggist put down the Telecomo. "Sergeant, you have a message. It is from General Artist Intichew. He says it is sealed and marked secret."

"Thank him and tell him we will be right there."

"The sergeant says thank you, He will be right there. Not at all."

"Thank you sir, that was a big help"

"It was my pleasure, Sergeant."

The four left the drug store, walked to the steps that led down to the latel docks.

"We have to run," said sergeant Beckwith.

"I guess so. You don't want to keep the general waiting." Said the redhead. "I think it's thrilling".

"Will I see you in a videdeck?" asked Star.

"Maybe. No, I don't think so. Come on private Culpepper, we have to run". "Will you come back to the Peabody?" Star asked.

"We can try to get back," said the sergeant."

The red-haired girl reached in the pack she had brought with her, got out two twisty, multi- colored candles; handed one to the private, one to the sergeant, saying, "I want you to have a gift from me. When you burn them, be sure my soul is simply glowing for you. Come back; if not today, when you can.. If we shouldn't be there, ask the lady there how you can contact Star and Deen. I'll bum candles for your safety".

The sergeant said "Thanks Deen. Goodbye, goodbye Star".

He and the private descended the steps to the docks, got in a latel. The sergeant set the dials. The latel glided through the pale light of the white tunnels, silent except for distant echoings. The light flicked over them in a shadowy effect as they passed under arch after arch. The pale white grayness of the tunnel ended in the blue light of the Histafu House dock. The soldiers stepped from the latel, the sergeant pushed a button and they rose to a sound of falling water. In the patio, Mr. Barfog was standing by a waterfall. He came over, handed out an envelope. The sergeant took out a slip of paper.

"They want us to be at the Walters tomorrow morning. Nothing extra secret about that," said the sergeant.

"It concerns the movement of a general," said Mr. Barfog.

"True. Yeah, in a way, a general is always at the front," said the sergeant.

"I'm glad to see you here, Private Culpepper. I'm Mr. Barfog. If I may, I would show you what we have for you." The two of them walked off.

Sergeant Beckwith turned a levitation control, rose to his room, went in, undressed, slipped into a robe; then, fixed a light screen so he could see the city through the outside wall; not clear, but as if the city were in a mist.

He curled up on the bed and opened his book. A story unfolded for him as he turned page after page. Outside, the sky got dark

The sergeant got off the bed and went to the telecomo.

"Good evening. I hope the German dinner pleased you."

"It did. Tonight I'll try the Far East." The lady suggested "China?"

"No. I think, Bourang. Tell the chef to select for me, and thanks." Back to his book he selected another story.

The bald man, in the dark suit, entered, put the supper tray on the table, left.

The sergeant got off the bed, used the toilet, washed; then he walked over and sat at his table, ate the exotic Bourang dishes. He finished drinking his tea, got up and adjusted his light screen. He took off his robe and put his B uniform back on, left his room and dropped to the patio. Mr. Barfog sat by the pool. He got up.

"Good evening, Mr. Barfog. Is Private Culpepper in his room?"

"No, I think he's at the Harwood. He seemed pleased with every thing I showed him. Then he seemed rather anxious and said he had to go home. I thought probably, in consideration for the clerk there, he wanted to pick up his notice from the general. But he hasn't returned."

"I thought of that. The old gentleman over there might have been worried. Then perhaps ⸻ ❧ ⸻ eabody Bookshop. We were there this afternoon."

"I enjoy the Peabody myself. I'd be interested in knowing how you discovered it. But let me check the Harwood and see if we can reach him there."

Mr. Barfog got his telecomo. "Good evening. This is Mr. Barfog of Histafu House. Is Private Culpepper in his room? He is. One second please."

Mr. Barfog told the sergeant, "He is in his room and the clerk will go fetch him if we wish."

"No, he's three floors up. The house como is obviously out of order. No, if he comes down have him wait for me."

"Sir," said Mr. Barfog, "You needn't do that, but if the private should come down, please have him wait there for the sergeant. Thank you sir."

"Thank you Mr. Barfog, I'll go right over."

The sergeant lowered himself to the docks, boarded a latel, set the dials, floated into the pale tunnels. The late! floated through the pale light, docked. He got out, climbed the steps, walked down the street, turned on the next street and walked up to the Harwood. He went in, walked up three floors and knocked. "Come in," said the private.

The sergeant entered. A candle sat burning on a square, spindly legged table. The room smelled faintly of incense. The candle threw wavery shadows everywhere. Private Culpepper sat in a straight chair, by the wall, reading his book. He was half in the waving shadow of an old round top piece of furniture. The doors on it standing open

150

showed the private's coat hanging on a hanger inside. The light of the candle flickered off an old dusty bureau; off the marble of a marble topped cabinet; off the brass bed, throwing shadows of the bed onto the wall behind it. Private Culpepper melted in and out of shadow as he read. His face looked all dark hollows.

"What are you doing here?" sergeant Beckwith asked.

"Reading my book."

"You could read that anytime. We could be talking to those pretty girls at the Bookshop or going to see what some of the other places are like."

The private kept on reading.

"Suit yourself, but remember that we only had a week. One day got shot to blazes at that jetport and we used a second day getting here and settled and all. Now this third day nearly done. That leaves tomorrow, then just two days before the day we have to go back. Come on, let's go somewhere."

"I'm a stayin here."

"Up to you. That's your choice. But God Damn turn on that lamp over there before you ruin your eyes. It's dark in here. See you in the momin' ." The sergeant went out of the room.

"Well, God damn," he said as he walked down the dark stairway. He walked through the lobby, out into the dark street. Through the darkness he could see a couple of old men on the other side of the street. He walked up to the entrance of the latel) docks, down the steps. The sergeant boarded the latel, set the dials and floated through the tunnels to the docks of Histafu House. He deboarded, levitated to the patio.

"Mr. Barfog,' said the sergeant to the man standing by the pool. "You know what my friend's doing? He's in a shabby room sitting on a hard ass chair, reading a book by candle light."

"That's not such a foolish thing," said Mr. Barfog.

"Well. Well, good night sir."

"Goodnight sergeant," said Mr. Barfog.

The sergeant levitated, entered his room, removed his clothes and laid them out for the morning, used his latrine; then, he lay on his bed, opened his book, read until sleepiness overtook him and he dimmed the illumination to darkness, drifted into sleep.

The early sunlight filled the room, shown brightly on the glass toilet bowl, glistened off the crystal and mirror on the dresser and, outside covered the city, seen as though layers of fine bright mist; or, as the sketched in outlines of a city not really there. The sergeant adjusted the screen. The city vanished and was replaced by what seemed fields of light, almost a landscape in lights and half-lights. The landscape got brighter.

Sergeant Beckwith went into his latrine, brushed his teeth, shaved, used his toilet; then, back into his room, he jumped into his pool, splashed around in it as the room got brighter. He climbed out. Dried off and watched where the towel evaporated into the air. At his dresser he put on clean clothes; then, over to his uniforms, got out his B; then put it back and took down his A uniform; then, put it back and got the D uniform and put it on. He went to his telecomo and activated it.

"Good morning," said a youngish blond woman. "What would you like for breakfast?"

"Pancakes and sausage, thank you, and coffee." He picked up his book, sat in the chair by the table, continued the story he'd started. A man in a dark suit entered; a slender, gray haired man. The man put the silver breakfast tray on the table, on the table in front of the sergeant, left the room.

The sergeant ate, left the room, descended to the patio. A tall, slender man with longish dark hair and large spectacles with heavy dark rims, was standing by the pool. He looked up and smiled.

"Good morning, Sergeant Beckwith."

"Good morning. Where is Mr. Barfog this morning?"

"Mr. Barfog has taken the day off. I'm Mr. Rahashinda. I'm filling in today." "Do you gentlemen more or less alternate in performing this office?"

"No. A number of us, who are more or less regular customers, take turns filling in for the help to give them breathing spells. Today is amateur day at a couple of posts. In the dining room Vane Swing has taken over for Dinny Grow. That was Vane who took your breakfast order. Dinny and Mr. Barfog are out at the water today."

"I understand, from the people I was with yesterday, that this hotel is a most difficult place to get into. They sounded most impressed when I said I was staying here."

"That's partly truth and partly myth. This is an expensive place in which to stay, but not nearly as much so as most people believe it is. It is no more expensive than many another vacation which a person with an average income will save for. The cost of upkeep for the house isn't high. There is almost no repair work needed here. The building, sturdier than the strongest steel structure, has a mere skeleton of glass arches for an exterior. There are no inside walls whatsoever. Did you realize that? If you go up into the towers, you will realize that it is one of the tallest buildings in the city, and there are no interior walls whatsoever. This is one of the buildings constructed by a rather famous group of rich and talented scientists and architects. Their best known project is the building in Wivenhue Park, a real art masterpiece inside and out. Nor is this place so exclusive as people are inclined to believe. There are many whom we would welcome who would never dream they would be accepted here. The only requirement is that one must have modeled his lifestyle after the teachings of Jankwar Sing. Those who have not would probably be happier in a more greatly structured situation."

"But I've never heard of Jankwar Sing."

"Most here haven't."

"How were we admitted?"

'Through your life, you have conducted yourselves according to the principles of Jankwar Sing. If you had not, you would have been directed to another hotel. The basic things which Sing says: Love life; love your fellow man; understand good sense in human relationships."

"It seems so simple. I'd better be off. I don't want to keep General Intichew waiting."

Sergeant Beckwith lowered himself to the docks, boarded a latel, floated into the white tunnel, through a tunnel to the dock near Harwood Hotel. He de-boarded, climbed the steps, walked down the street. Here and there, weeds were coming up through the cracks in the sidewalk. He walked down to the comer and turned, past some trash which lay about; a couple old dirty newspapers, a bent rusted beer container. He entered the Harwood. He nodded to the desk clerk, walked up the stairs, knocked on Private Culpepper's door.

"Come in," called a voice. Private Culpepper sat in a chair by the window, looking up to where the gray clouds fled through the gray-blue sky. The light of the morning sun fell on the paintless window frames and on the gray dusty floorboards.

"Ready to go? Come on. Let's go see the man," said the sergeant.

Private Culpepper got up. The soldiers left the room, went down the stairs. "Good morning," said the sergeant to the desk clerk.

"Good morning, sir," said the clerk.

The soldiers walked up toward the docks.

"They tell me the customers do a lot of the work at the Histafu." I think I'll volunteer you as kitchen help; you aren't doing anything particular. Seriously, I think I'll volunteer to spend a day working in the kitchen, or perhaps getting a vacant room ready for inspection. It might be fun."

They descended the dock steps, boarded a latel. The sergeant took the list from his pocket, the Histafu list of restaurants, clubs, places of interest. He looked at it, then set the latel dial for the Walters. The latel sailed through a tunnel, turned, sailed through a tunnel, docked. The soldiers got out, went up stairs, and they were in the lobby of the Walters. A uniformed guard showed them into a room full of men who were standing around a large central table. Between them and the table was a gray, dusty trunk. In one comer, the general; a large wide-faced man with his hair cut close to the top of his head. He looked down at the soldiers and laughed.

"Doesn't that beat all hell? Men, you crossed us up," said the general. "The major here said he bet you would come see me spit and polished in your A's. I said not so. The sergeant, with the history of being a very combatty fellow will be in battle dress for this mission. The private, a record as a hard-working fellow with a trend away from ostentatious display, will come in his normal pass uniform, his B. Here I see him ready to go into battle. The sergeant, however, treats this as it is, a work meeting, and comes in D work dress. I compliment you both on your choice. The four of us show the non-military individuals a showcase display of military dress. The major in dress B, the sergeant in work dress D, the private in battle dress C, I in field dress E."

"The general thinks of this as a sporting occasion," said the major. The men laughed, the general, loudest of all.

"Men, may I introduce myself and the others of our team. I'm General Intichew, President of Lamar S.I. With me are Dr. Roper and Major Halstead, both of Lamar. This is Dr. Dimichef of M.I.T., Dr. Armstrong of Virginia Beach Research Lab, Dr. Ftah of Rine E.S.I., Dr. Zipfud of Shizolt Sprang Institute, Dr. Smarslit of Einstein Hall, and you have met Dr. Rhodes. I hope you aren't feeling ill, Private Culpepper."

The sergeant looked over at his friend.

Private Culpepper's face had gone colorless. Gray shadows seemed to be on it from some place.

"I was a young man myself, I hope I may say not too long ago. And the parties, many long into the night, and the drinks went around, and the drinks went 'round. And the last thing I wanted to do was get up and be present for duty the next morning. But that's the life of a soldier, and we soldiers always make it."

Private Culpepper's face seemed to be splotched with dark purple.

"Roper, here, and Smarslit and Zipfud, were here all day yesterday with their instruments, testing and peeking into the trunk. Do you suppose I might be granted a tiny peek into it before you gentlemen start on your reports? You see, I just got here," said the general.

"It won't hurt a thing in the world," said Dr. Roper, a curly-haired gentleman of medium height with a large square jaw.

The sergeant looked at Private Culpepper. The private's face was blotched in purplish shadows seeming almost transparent; his jacket seemed charred in the center. The sergeant looked again. The charred spot wasn't there. It was only the shadows.

The general walked over to the box. The general continued, "This box is so old and dusty, it might be one of those antique art objects itself." He laughed.

There was a burnt spot on Culpepper's jacket. In the jacket was a charred hole, and his flesh was burnt away. And his charred bones were showing.

The general opened the box. A stench came out. "There's a dead man in the box," he said. He looked up.

The sergeant looked over at Culpepper. Culpepper wasn't there.

"Where did the private go?" said the general. "Did he faint? Did he bug out?"

"Sir, I think he's in the box. The Germans shot him and put him there four days ago,"

"Malarkey," said the general loudly. He looked at the body in the box. The major came over, lifted up his head.

"Somehow, General," said the major, "that might be true."

"Alright, let's find a possible scientific explanation of what we have tested in the box becoming what we now see in the box, plus the possibility that it is the private whom we saw before us who is now in the box. So, let's get cracking," said the general.

A tall thin gentleman with wavy gray hair and rimless spectacles, walked up to the box, looked in.

"I'm Dr. Armstrong," he said. "Sergeant Beckwith, if you please, would you go over with us the events in sufficient detail, exactly what took place four days ago; then, bring us up to date as far as you can. Then we can compare your rendition of events with the scientific reports which have been made. The major can help out or fill in as it seems to him appropriate to do so. First, give a brief, very brief, account to help us get our bearing."

The sergeant began. "First, the first part is about technical and secret weap onry. General Intichew, sir, may I get some help from you and the major in explaining the new device which we were using when we discovered the trunk?"

"Certainly. That's very wise, Sergeant. Let me begin by saying I'm going to describe the Armed Forces' most secret gadget. If anyone here would particularly like to absent himself, he may at this point.

If not, we are all co-holders of some most secret information. We scientists have developed an advanced matter projector. We know of crude and limited ones which were of no value to the military, of little value to anybody, except as test guinea pigs. This new one, just the reverse is true. We plan to use it to break the war stalemate. First, it will project humans through space at the speed of light and with no discernible ill effects to them at all. Second, it will project an intelligent shadow of a person to a designated place to arrive well ahead of his remaining physical matter. This shadow can take a look see and withdraw completely if the place is unsafe. Or it can withdraw, make adjustments according to the situation, then return. Now, Sergeant."

"General, if I may, sir, perhaps I should make a couple of introductory state ments," said the major. "There were some things which I _didn't explain to the sergeant because I was testing a weapon, not explaining a weapon to our enlisted personnel, and I wanted to keep some of its potentialities under wrap. I hadn't explained what we call an anticipation setting. The sergeant hit on it by accident. When I saw no sergeant at the target area, I figured he might have hit an anticipation number, so I set mine on a wunt. The sergeant was on a two. In our testing of anticipation settings, an object projected at those settings would almost never be detected without the use of specialized equipment. There are, however, some individuals who have developed in themselves a type of extrasensory perception which would allow them to perceive a person who is on an anticipation projection. The individuals with this sense are extremely rare. However, the first German sensed us and fired at me. Then Culpepper perceived us and crawled out of the trench before we were yet actually at that location."

The sergeant interrupted. "Sir, do you mean we were spiritually, but not materially, at that location.

"You might say so. Of course, as I understand it, spirit is a matter of a type," said the major. "The forward projection is matter, but it is not the matter which is the physically functioning you. On this anticipation setting, we are doing what is scientifi cally known as ghosting."

"But you said Culpepper crawled out of the trench," said the sergeant. "On our settings we both saw him. But I switched settings

157

and went right back and saw Culpepper not out of the trench, but in the trench, and the Germans shot him and put him in the trunk. Then you came and shot the Germans," said Sergeant Beckwith.

"Then that's the answer," said Dr. Armstrong. "Culpepper, with the strong belief that he was saved, with the power of his will, spiritually crawled from the trench; then, enough physical matter followed to maintain a physical presence out of the trunk until it became necessary for him to face squarely the hard fact that he was going to see his physical self where it had been shot and thrown. His sense of logic caused a breakdown in his belief that he was physically out of the trunk. And as he refuted that belief, his physical matter was drawn into the trunk in the condition in which you now see him. If you remember, Sergeant, it was you, not he, who actually saw him shot and thrown into the trunk. He was spiritually outside the trench.

"That's right, he was behind me and the major."

"So he never could be quite sure until he was forced to see inside the trunk," said Dr. Armstrong.

"Culpepper was doing what is, in an old-fashioned way, known as ghosting," said Dr. Ftah.

"Well, that about wraps it up," said the general.

"May I ask one question?" said Dr. Zipfud. "Sergeant, when you and the major were together in the trench, why did you not tell him of seeing a body thrown into the trunk?"

"Let me have a shot at that question, Dr. Zipfud," said the general. "It would have been rare indeed should a sergeant, pass in hand, have eyesight enough to have seen an odd thing which might have impeded his impending trip. A good sergeant sees about a quarter of what he sees anyway. Stupid corporals see things sometimes. You can bet on some sharp-eyed private to see a thing out of order, tell his smart-assed, bucking lieutenant all about it, the lieutenant put it on a report. Then some captain or major would have signed it, so he wouldn't get his ass in a jam, and unless some sage colonel caught hold of it, by some accident dropped his cigar on it, it would have caused mounds of trouble all up and down the line."

"Then, too, Doctor," said the sergeant, "on line one sees funny things. Some, tired eyes; some, out of hand imagination. Up front can be a pretty strange place."

"Sergeant, finish your pass. Then report to me at Lamar. I don't want to chance getting you captured. Will you accept the rank of Lieutenant?"

"Yes sir."

"Then consider yourself promoted. Your uniforms will be changed to officer's uniforms by the time you get back to your hotel."

"Thank you sir."

"So, Lieutenant Beckwith, report."

"Lieutenant Beckwith reporting as ordered, sir."

The general returned his salute. "Very good, Lieutenant. Carry on."

Major Halstead shook his hand. "Lieutenant, let me be the first to congratulate you."

"Thank you, Major Halstead. Major, may I ask; I didn't want to dwell on this part of the inquiry, in front of everybody, that I, a sergeant, should have accidentally hit the button, thus taking a chance on screwing up the whole detail. But I'm still puzzled. When I hit that button, why you should have been changing weapons. You saw the Merekin crawl out of the trench and get behind us. That should have left only the old box in the trench. How did you know he was still in the trench?"

"Lieutenant, I never saw him crawl out. You remember, we were on different anticipation settings. You, on a two, saw a spirit happening take place which I, on a one, never saw. Two is, of course, that much closer to pure spirit. And I didn't think of it at the time; neither the German nor Culpepper gave any evidence of having seen you. I, on wunt, would have been much more easily perceived. It was I at whom the German fired. Then, when I got back to the trench, Culpepper's body had been shot, had relaxed its hold on physical matter, and his free spirit had already drawn much of the matter back to it. When you returned on setting zero, if you remember, you never saw the free spirit."

The lieutenant asked, "Majro Halstead, why would you not use

159

another anticipation than wunt, which is the most easily perceived?"

"There are problems with ghosting at two or thuree. Because of certain mechanical failures which are likely to occur at thuree, we would, in a tactical situation, seldom use that setting. We might use it if there were ghosting detecting devices being used against us. In using the projection device, one encounters a host of complex problems. You'll find out all about them when you get to Lamar."

"Congratulations, Lieutenant," said Dr. Rhodes. "Congratulations," said Dr. Ftah. They shook hands.

"Dr. Ftah," said the lieutenant. "Why do you suppose Culpepper came back with me to the Walters?"

"Force of the authority which he was trained to obey. Maybe, too, he needed the answer to his own question. In any case, he would surely have reported back for duty. He likely would never have returned from the war; been reported missing, his body never found, sort of faded away, it would have."

"There've been similar cases to Culpepper's, haven't there? What happens to them?" asked the lieutenant.

"Oh, yes," said Dr. Ftah. "They turn up in odd places. Some call them faded people. There was a monk in an ancient, forgotten monastery, believed so strongly in life that for ages his physical body refused to die. It continued to petform life's rituals after its vital organs, heart, lungs, stomach, had ceased to function. The last I visited that monastery, Brother Mrawthrup, that was the monk's name, had been kneeling at prayer for several years, and no one disturbed him. The other monks thought that he might again rise and speak. And other monks of that same monastery gave indication that they were passing into a state similar to Brother Mrawthrup's. Sometimes tramps who have no ceremonial burial to cement the idea of death into their spirits may wander a long time in a state which is something less than life. They have less physical self to maintain. Then, in worn out sections of cities, the men on the skid rows, a number of them, get grayer and grayer. Then one day, there are just a few tattered rags in a comer. Of all the old men on the skid rows, you don't hear of all that many bodies being found, do you? I thought not."

The roaring voice of the general said, "Now, that's what I mean about reports. We've got to list him as dead as of now or be ready to explain that for four days, he was just ghosting. You can bet some busy-body will run his mouth, wondering why that fatal wound wasn't apprehended and treated at some time during those four days."

"And think of the things we've had him do," said the major. "We'll have to give him a medal for devotion to duty while suffering from a massive wound."

"You've got it, Major," roared the general. "We'll give him a silver star; assisting in the capture and securing of a priceless work of art, daylight hazards of no man's land and all that, and safe transport to final destination. What work of art? That old trunk there has just appeared to me exquisitely beautiful. Then, the lieutenant here gets a bronze medal, bravery in the petformance of hazardous duty, assisting in the capture of trunk, and so forth. That will give me reason for having promoted him without the usual whoop-de-doo and folderol. We have an awards parade to further the spirit of patriotism in the city of Baltimore, pictures in vidibells, newspapers, telereels, all the media. Dr. Rhodes present in behalf of the Walters Gallery, acceptance, grati tude, and the rest of that crap. Then the doctor gives the trunk to the Virginia Beach Research Lab for further study. Then Virginia Beach ships it someplace; Atlantis would be just fine. We'll need a not over-bright private to sign papers as awards witness.

Lieutenant, come up with a name. You know the whole trouble with the army?" roared the general. "It's too many sharp-ass privates who see things and too many bucking-ass lieutenants who fill out reports. O.K., Lieutenant, a name."

"Private Henley, the hellis driver, sir."

"Private Henly it is. And it would be alright if he didn't know a hell of a lot about what he's signing. What the hell does he care anyway? All he has to do is sign it. Tell him it's part of his trip ticket. No problem. All of a sudden, I'll get extremely interested in all the details of how this exquisite art thing came to Mereka. My inquisi tiveness will add up to pages and pages, the details the Walters Gallery will need for its permanent records. There will be mounds of bullshit for him to sign. I've done all the work, found out all the information. All he needs to do is sign, sign, sign. He'll begin to realize he's shipped a pretty valuable item. Private Henley'll think he's shipped the bust of Paulmoll. And we have what we need tucked in very nicely among the bullshit. And Private Henley signs the son-of-a-bitch, and there's an end to it."

THE BIG PROBLEM

The road took the reporter into Ellicott City. He drove to the center of town. People were running toward the courthouse. The reporter stopped his car. On an old stone bench outside the courthouse a glum old man was seated. The reporter asked the glum man what the problem was.

"The Sun's burning out."

"Is that all that's worrying people?"

"No, the Galaxy's flying apart."

"Is that all?"

"That's enough," said the glum man.

163

A Fragment of the Shadow

. . . and the day was darkening, the grey sky filled with dark clouds, darkest in front of them. They sped down the dusty, patched macadam road. In front of them, in the sky, a vague flash of light lit the darkness.

"Looks like we're heading into it. I hope we get there before," the woman was saying to the grim driver.

They sped on, passing weeds, nettles, dusty leaved shrubs. Weed filled meadows undulated up and down.

"Will we know? I mean, when we are there?"

"Try to spot a road sign," said the man, his eyes on the road ahead of him, "We are bound to come to one eventually."

They sped on past weeds and undulating fields. "We already passed one, but couldn't read it." "We were going too fast."

"We aren't likely to be going any slower," said the woman, watching out the window, her eyes on the undulating fields.

"And the road sign was in shadow."

The woman did not reply, only watched the greyed fields rise and fall as the car sped onward.

The tree covered hills along the far horizons were cloaked in the mists of the fading light. A few old fence posts and a grey warped gate appeared at the edge of a field, fled past them and were gone. Dusty leaved shrubs passed by in an unbroken line. Ahead, the man could see a fork in the road.

"Well, which way do we go?"

The woman looked to the front. "Let's take the left this time." "The left it is."

They headed for the fork ahead, the place where the road passed to either side of a wedge of dusty bushes, the surface of each way seeming equally patched, equally old. They headed down the left branch, or tine, of the fork. The wedge of dusty shrubs and trees gave way and there, on the flat side of the road, was a little old man in a red cap. He wore grey, baggy trousers, a yellowed shirt and his whiskers nearly of a length to be called a beard.

"Now that man's going to get wet if it should storm. Let's do stop and give him a lift."

The car pulled to a stop just past the man with the little red cap. He ran to the car.

"Hop in the back there," the driver said.

The door slammed. They again moved forward down the road. The side of the road was covered with dusty weeds and nettles. They moved under a dark sky, through the fading light. The clouds to the front were darkest. There was a flicker of light in the clouds ahead of them. "Looks like it might storm."

The man didn't reply. He watched the road in front of him. The woman turned her head and watched out the side window, watched the undulating fields of greyed weeds. Clumps of dusty shrubs passed by.

"Will we know?"

"What?"

"When we get there," the woman explained.

The man said nothing for a minute, watched the brown patchy road ahead.

"Seems I saw a road sign back a ways,"

"But it was in shadow," she reminded him.

"So it was."

The man watched the dusty brown road, bumped over grey road patches. Tall dusty weeds and low shrubs passed by on either side. A couple of spindly trees slid past and were lost in the distance behind. Dusty shrubs accumulated on either side of the road. On they went in silence. The woman looked out the side window to watch the greyed, darkening undulating fields. The tree covered hills along the far horizons were cloaked in the mists of the fading light. Dusty leaves of shrubs passed by in an unbro ken line. Ahead, the man could see a fork in the road.

"Well, which way do we go?" The woman looked to the front.

"Let's take the left this time."

"The left it is."

They headed for the fork ahead, the place where the road passed to either side of a wedge of dusty bushes, the surface of each way seeming equally patched, equally old. They headed down the left tine of the fork. The wedge of dusty shrubs and trees gave way and there, on the flat side of the road, was a little old man in a red cap. He wore grey batty trousers and his shirt was yellowed and dirty. On his face were long, unkept whiskers.

"It's like to rain and that man's going to get wet. Let's do stop and give him a lift."

The car pulled to a stop just past the man. He ran up to the car. "Hop in the back there," the driver said.

The door slammed. They again moved forward down the road. The side of the road was covered with dusty weeds and nettles. They moved under a dark sky, through the fading light. The clouds to the front were darkest. Up in the clouds there was a faint flash of light.

"Looks like it might storm."

The man didn't reply. He watched the road in front of him. The woman turned her head and watched out the side window, watched the darkening, undulating fields. Clumps of dusty shrubs passed.

"Wonder where the children are?" the woman mumbled, mostly to herself.

"God knows."

"That's good," she said in a mumbled whisper, "That's good." She looked out the window and watched the shrubs pass by.

The man watched the dusty brown road, bumped over grey road patches. Dusty weeds and low shrubs were mingled together on either side of the road. A couple of clumps of tall shrubs slid past. Out the side window the woman watched the darken ing hilly fields;

166

the dark, rock and shrub filled depressions. The tree covered hills along the far horizons were cloaked in the mists of fading light. Dusty leafed shrubs passed by in an unbroken line. Ahead, the man could see a fork in the road.

"Well, which way do we go." The woman looked to the front.

"Let's take the left this time."

"The left it is."

They headed for the fork ahead, the place where the road passed to either side of a wedge of dusty bushes, the surface of each way seeming equally patched, equally old. They headed down the left tine of the fork. The wedge of dusty shrubs and trees gave way and there, on the flat side of the road, was a little old man in a red cap. He wore grey baggy trousers and a dirty, yellowed shirt. Long whiskers covered his face.

"It's likely to rain, those clouds, that man will get wet. We could stop and give him a lift."

The car pulled to a stop just past the man. The man ran up to the car. "Hop in the back there," the driver said.

The door slammed. They again moved forward down the road. The side of the road was covered with dusty weeds and nettles. They moved under a dark sky, through the fading light. The clouds to the front were darkest. There was a pale flash of light in the clouds ahead.

"Looks like a storm ahead,"

The man didn't reply. He watched the road in front of him. The woman turned her head and watched out the side window. The greyed fields rose and fell as she watched. A clump of dark shrubs passed.

"Seems to me I've seen that man before."

"What? What man?" The driver watched the road ahead as he spoke.

"You know, the red hat."

The man didn't reply. He watched the dusty brown road, uneven at the edges; bumped over grey road patches. Low, weedy shrubs passed by on either side. Taller shrubs accumulated on either side of the road. On they went in silence. The woman looked out the side window, watched the darkening, undulating fields. The tree covered hills along the far horizon were shrouded by the fading light. An unbroken line of dusty leafed shrubs were passing. Ahead, the man could see a fork in the road.

"Well, which way do we go?"

The woman looked to the front.

"Let's take the left this time."

"The left it is."

They headed for the fork ahead, the place where the road passed to either side of a wedge of dusty bushes, the surface of each way seeming equally patched, equally old. They headed down the left tine of the fork. The wedge of dusty shrubs and trees gave way and there, on the flat side of the road, was a little old man in a red cap. His grey trousers were baggy and his shirt, dirty and yellowed. Long, unkept whiskers covered his face.

"It's likely to rain and that man will get wet. Do let's stop and give him a lift."

The car pulled to a slop just past the man. The man ran up to the car.

"Hop in the back there," the driver said.

The door slammed. They again moved forward down the road. The side of the road was covered with dusty weeds and nettles. They moved under a dark sky, through fading light. The clouds to the front were the darkest. The clouds to the front lit up briefly.

"Looks like it might storm."

The man didn't reply. He watched the road in front of him. The woman turned her head, to watch out the side window. She watched the undulating fields, dark in the hollows. Dusty clumps of shrubs passed by. Here was grey stand, partly fallen into the weeds and on it, three rusting milk cans. It slipped past.

"It's comforting."

"What?"

"To see something man made."

"And this road's not man made?" the driver asked. "Make sense." He stared at the road ahead, drove on.

"No, that's not it." mumbled the woman.

The car sped forward. The woman looked out the window, watched the dusty shrubs pass by. The man watched the dusty brown road, bumped over grey road patches. Along the side of the road were dusty weeds and low shrubs. Clumps of tall shrubs slid past. Out the side window, the woman watched the darkening, undulating fields. The tree covered hills along the far horizons were cloaked in the mists of fading light. Dusty leafed shrubs passed by in an unbroken line. Ahead, the man could see a fork in the road.

"Well, which way do we go?" "Let's take the left this time." "The left it is."

They headed for the fork ahead, the place where the read passed to either side of a wedge of dusty bushes, the surface of each way seeming equally patched, equally old. They headed down the left tine of the fork. The wedge of dusty trees and shrubs gave way and there, on the flat side of the road was a little old man in a red cap. He wore grey baggy trousers and a dirty shirt and whiskers covered his face.

"It's threatening to rain. That man is sure to get wet. We could stop and give him a lift."

The car pulled to a stop just past the man. The man ran up to the car. "Hop in the back there," the driver said.

The door slammed. They again moved forward down the road. The side of the road was covered with dusty weeds and nettles. They moved under a dark sky, through the fading light. The clouds to the front were the darkest. There was a pale, brief illumination of the clouds ahead.

"Looks like a storm brewing ahead of us".

The man didn't reply. He watched the road in front of him. The woman turned her head to watch out the side window. There was a gentle rolling of the darkening fields which fled past the car. Clumps of tall, slender shrubs slid past.

"I'm worried about darkness catching us." "What? It's dark

already."

"I mean the stars and all that," the woman mumbled.

They sped on. The woman glumly watched the dusty, darkening shrubs, taller here. They bumped over grey patches in the uneven road. Taller shrubs stood in long patches beyond the weeds and low shrubs. They rode on in silence. The tree covered hills along the far horizons were shrouded in the mists of failing light. There were passing an unbroken line of dusty leafed shrubs. Ahead, the man could see a fork in the road.

"Well, which way do we go?" The woman looked to the front. "Let's take a left this time,"

"The left it is,"

They headed for the fork ahead, the place where the road passed to either side of a wedge of dusty bushes. The surface to either side of the wedge seemed equally patched, equally old. They headed down the left tine of the fork. The wedge of dusty shrubs and trees gave way and there, on a flat side of the road, was a little old man in a red cap. He wore baggy grey trousers and his shirt was yellowed and dirty. Long whiskers were all over his face.

"It looks like it's gonna rain and that man will get wet. We could stop and give him a ride."

The car pulled to a stop just past the man. The man ran up to the car.

"Hop in the back there," the driver said.

The door slammed. They again moved forward down the road. The sides of the road were covered with nettles and dusty weeds. Undulating, darkening fields stretched out to either side. They rode under a dark sky, through fading light. The clouds to the front were the darkest. There was a flicker of light in the clouds ahead.

"Looks like a storm coming on."

The man didn't reply. He watched the road in front of him. The woman turned her head and watched out the side window. The darkening fields dipped and sank, little hills and hollows. Clumps of dust covered shrubs passed by.

"And will we know? I forget."

The man, eyes on the road, drove on in silence. The woman turned her head. "I mean, what you said."

The man drove silently on. The woman turned back to the side window, watched the rise and fall of the darkening fields. Low weedy shrubs passed by. The woman watched the dark, undulating fields. The tree covered hills along the far horizon were cloaked in the darkening mist of fading light. An unbroken line of dusty leafed shrubs stretched along the side of the road. Ahead, the man could see a fork in the road.

"Well, which way do we go?" The woman looked to the front.

"Let's take the left this time,"

"The left it is,"

They headed for the fork ahead, the place where the road passed to either side of a wedge of dusty bushes, the surface of the road to either side of the wedge seeming equally old, equally patched. They headed down the left tine of the fork. The wedge of dusty shrubs and trees gave way and there, on the flat side of the road, was a little old man in a red cap. He wore grey baggy pants and a yellowed shirt. Unkept whiskers covered his face.

"It looks like a storm and that man will get wet. Let's stop and give him a ride."

The car pulled to a stop just past the man. The man ran up to the car. "Hop in the back there," the driver said.

The door slammed. They again moved forward down the road. The side of the road was covered with dusty weeds and nettles. They moved under a dark sky, through the fading light. The clouds to the front were darkest. There was a faint flash of light in the clouds ahead of them.

"Looks like it might storm."

The man didn't reply. He watched the road in front of him. The woman turned her head to watch out the side window, watch the dusty weeds, bunches of tall yellowed grasses, scraggly shrubs with dusty leaves. Beyond the dusty shrubs and weeds at the roadside, the darkening fields rose up and down in undulating folds. Shrubs, in a hedge row, fled past.

"I worry about getting there and all." "What?"

"I do, I worry about it," the woman mumbled. "What?"

"I mean getting there."

"What?"

The man drove on watching the dirty road, frayed at the edges. Tall dusty weeds and low shrubs passed by on either side. They rode silently onward, the woman watching out the side window, watching the greyed, undulating fields. The tree covered hills along the horizon were cloaked in the dusk of fading light. Dusty shrubs passed by in an unbroken line. Ahead, the man could see a fork in the road.

"Well, which way do we go?" The woman looked to the front. "Let's take the left this time."

"The left it is."

They headed for the fork ahead, the place where the road passed to either side of a wedge of dusty bushes. The surface each way seemed equally patched, equally old. They headed down the left tine of the fork. The wedge of dusty shrubs and trees gave way and there, on the flat side of the road, was a little old man in a red cap. His grey trousers were baggy and his yellowed shirt, dirty. Long scraggly whiskers covered his face giving, somewhat, an impression of a beard.

"It's likely getting ready to rain and that man's going to get wet. Oh, let's stop and give him a lift."

The car pulled to a stop just past the man. He ran up to the car. "Hop in the back there," the driver said.

The door slammed. They again moved forward down the road. The side of the road was covered with dusty weeds and nettles. They moved under a dark sky, through fading light. The clouds to the front were darkest. Up in the clouds ahead of them there was a flicker of light.

"Looks like it might storm."

The man didn't reply. He watched the road in front of him. The woman turned er head to watch out the side window. She watched the darkening, undulating fields. Clumps of dusty shrubs passed.

"Wonder where the children are?" mumbled the woman. "What?"

The woman looked out the window. Clumps of shrubs passed.

The man watched the dusty brown road, patched and ragged at the edges. Dusty weeds and low shrubs were mingled on either side of the road. Beyond the shrubs here were some grey, bramble covered fence posts. They slid past. The woman watched, out of the side window, the little hilly fields, darkening in the fading light, rise up and down. The tree covered hills along the far horizons were shrouded in mists of fading light. Dusty leaved shrubs passed by in an unbroken line. Ahead, the man could see a fork in the road.

"Well, which way do we go?"

The woman looked to the front. "Let's take the left this time."

"The left it is."

They headed for the fork ahead, the place where the road passed to either side of a wedge of dusty bushes. The surface of the road each way seemed equally old, equally patched. They headed down the left tine of the fork. The wedge of dusty shrubs and trees gave way and there, on the flat side of the road, was a little old man in a red cap. He wore baggy grey pants and a shirt that was rumpled and dirty, and his face was covered with long, scraggly, shaggy whiskers.

"It seems like it's going to rain. That man will get wet. Oh let's give him a lift. Let's stop and... "

The car pulled to a stop just past the man. The man ran up to the car. "Hop in the back there," the driver said.

The door slammed. They again moved forward down the road. The roadsides were covered with dusty weeds. They moved under a dark sky, through the fading light. The dark sky was covered with dark clouds. The clouds ahead were darkest. There was a pale flicker in the clouds ahead of them.

"Looks like a storm ahead."

The man didn't reply. He watched . . .

The Doors of Henvelyn

Said Bran, "You may take my head with you to the hall at
Henvelyn And there ye may feast the years away
And my head shall be as good company to you
As ever it was when on my shoulders
And the birds of Rhiannon shall sing to you also
So that you shall know no trouble, nor ailment.
But you must not open that door toward the sea;
For if you open that door, you must leave the hall
And the troubles of the world
Will again be your troubles."
So Manannan cut off the head of the blessed Bran
And they took the head with them
To the hall at Henvelyn.
In the wavery silvergrey mist,
Among the green vee and wye shadows of trees,
In the early winds of sunrise,
Singing fruit and flower sunrising songs,
The lemon birds sang
Till the mist, mixed with the wild singing,
Floated away from where flowers did nod,
Did nod on their stalks
In the wet push of the wind,
Did nod over scattered bones.
High above, sat Heilyn, the Impeller of the Sky,
Looking down through crystal windows
In the great hall.
Then spake Heilyn, "Sit we here feasting
While all these dead
Lie not, as they should, dark in their graves
Buried among their venerable ancestors?
Shame on my beard if I do not open that door."
The door flew open. The wind blew through
The grey dome of the sky and all the old

Troubles of the world fell upon those faces
Gathered in the hall at Henvelyn,
And the birds flew away.
And far off, over the cold waves of the sea,
The birds flew away.
And they took the head of the blessed Bran,
And after a long journey,
Buried it in White Hill.
And after it had been buried for many years,
King Arthur dug up the head
And he took the head of Bran
And he threw it out to the waters
So that the head floated away.

LOOKING BACKWARD WITH REGRETS

Now about the sword
And I've shed tears over that.
It was a beautiful sword and I
Wasn't thinking about my Lord
Needing it in the otherworld.
Then, I was a friend at last and
Loyal to my King — I am no harper
And will not sing high praises,
But will say there are true feelings
That flit across my heart.

I was there when the baby
Mordred Was put to sail - if sail it was for
There was no sail and it was little more
Than a wooden trunk.
I could understand Merlin's reason,
The stability of the land — still,
Mordred was a good man and if
I'd been Mordred, you understand —
But I am loyal may my beard
Fall from my face if I am not.

I was there when my Lord received
Lady Morgan's coat. No, it would not
Have tickled, but, he would not have
Died from it. The Lady, if she so desired,
She had the power to kill. Then, the
Maid who brought it, if the King had died,
She would have burned and Lady Morgan
Loved her I am sure of that. And I
Could not have sat and watched the
Maiden suffer had I been Lord, but I

Was loyal then as I am now. I
Could not move to save her. I
Say these things a harper would not say —
I am no harper. Those things fit not well
In song

I was there when my lovely Lady died —
Lancelot was guilty but in thought, not act.
A kiss was what my Lady wanted, nothing more,
And Lancelot's love was true to her desire.
My Lady took no pleasure in the physical —
Her pleasure was the purity of thoughts
And dreams. The King knew that.
He honoured her, then handled other bodies.
He was the nation's growing power. It was
His duty to express himself. He was
The land itself and I was loyal —
I am no harper to sing songs of praise,
But I can speak, I was loyal and
Can tell you that —
Then, after Baden,
Had I owned a harp,
Full half my fingers
Would have been hard put
Had they had a need
To touch the strings.

Note: As one recalls, Sir Bedevere lost a hand in the Battle of Mount Baden.

CUFF LINKS

Mr. Sidewall was looking for his cufflinks. He had looked simply everywhere he thought of. His wife, he knew would be standing by the front door, an exasperated look on her face.

"Come on Henry," came her voice up the stairs. ·

He had been wrong. She had moved to the bottom of the stairs. It was a little black box he was looking for. He searched again among the articles on his bedside table, searched through his things in his bureau drawers, top to bottom; searched the top of his wife's vanity, the floor around it. He searched the floor around the bureau, the wardrobe, searched the comers of the room; he got down on his stomach, searched through the rolls of dust under his bed.

Under his bed were little figures, like toy soldiers; only they weren't soldiers; they were like the people one sees under Christmas trees, peopling the villages around model railroads. Clearing some of the dust away with his hand, Mr. Sidewall discov ered he could not pick up any of the figures and examine it, because it was far below him. The floor had, in fact, given away under the bed and rocky cliffs dropped to a valley below. Mr. Sidewall crawled further under the bed, hung over the cliff. He was watching a funeral in progress. The pall bearers were carrying the casket from the house and the casket did look like the box his cuff links were in.

"There it is," he shouted, reached down and grabbed it, the coffin, the box with his cuff links in it.

He crawled out from under the bed.

"It's about time," said his wife; who was, by then, standing in the doorway gazing at him, "I was wondering what you were doing down there."

Mr. Sidewall opened the box, took out the cuff links. The cuff links were odd, things he had inherited: dark rectangles in which were carved, in each, a naked man; so small, it took close scrutiny to determine they were naked. Mr. Sidewall was now ready to take his wife to lunch. He put on his hat, then he and his wife went, together, out the front door.

After, and in spite of, the odd start; Mr. Sidewall enjoyed his day off from his job; his lunch with his wife and , after that, his afternoon spent working in his yard. He didn't get many days off during the week and for the next few weeks, his only time off was the habitual Saturday and Sunday. It was weeks later before he got a week day off and that was not a day he found much pleasure in; for, he had to visit his dentist. It was, in fact, a full year after the occurrence with the cuff links before he felt he could spare the time, on a week day, to take his wife to lunch. He dressed. He was all dressed except he had misplaced his hat. Thinking back, he thought he knew where it was; but thought that today he would go bareheaded. He waited at the front door for his wife.

She was in the bathroom, washing. Mr. Sidewall was glad he'd had the plumbers fix the drain yesterday. But what a mess that was. They had to go through the wall to get to the pipe. But here was his wife.

"Where is your hat?" "I misplaced it."

"You'll need to wear it, I can wait." "I'd rather go without it."

"No. I won't hear of it. Not one foot of mine goes out that door till you have your hat on your head."

There was no hope for it. Mr. Sidewall went upstairs. Again he took one hopeful look through the things in the closet. But he knew where it was. In that old, seldom used wardrobe. His wife must have put it in there. He went to the wardrobe; the dusty antique with the round, head shaped carving on its top and winglike decorations extending across the top and down the sides like reaching arms.

Mr. Sidewall opened his wardrobe doors. There was no back to the wardrobe, nor wall behind it.

"Strange", said Mr. Sidewall, with some annoyance: the plumbers couldn't have moved it. Look they didn't even fix the wall back."

He stepped inside to look. He was in a strange hall. It was a dark, long hall. "You found a place to put your hat?" called a voice.

"I put it in the wardrobe," he answered.

He turned. There was an old, antique wardrobe. He went up the hall toward the room from which he had heard the voice, there was a door to his right. He opened it and here was a parlour.

"Now come in Fred, and I'll pour your coffee," said the woman.

There were two other women in the room and another man. They were seated around a small fire and each held a cup of coffee. They looked somehow familiar.

"Fred, this is my cousin Clairey, whom you've heard me speak of so many times."

"How do you do, Clairey."

Fred was sure he had been in this room many times, but was it a dream, he was thinking he was someone else. He was Henry Sidewall. He knew all about himself. His wife was waiting by the door. But now that seemed dreamlike. Of course, he was Fred. Fred who? Fred Abernathy. Why, he wasn't even married.

"I don't recall that, Jack. But it doesn't lessen my pleasure at meeting this charming person."

Fred was still worried. His hostess: what was her name? And the other woman who kept giving him a strange look.

"You look worried, Fred. What on Earth ails you today," said that woman.

"It was only this strange dream I was having."

"Last night," asked the hostess.

"No, day dream."

"Since you've been here?" asked that other woman.

"I think so."

Fred drank coffee; got a refill; tried to listen to the conversation carefully, so that he could take some part in it. He still was convinced he got here through a wardrobe. The other woman beside the hostess: Jack called her Alice. Of course, he knew Alice. But who Alice was, he couldn't think. Clairey said she had to be going. Alice said she, also, should be leaving.

"Jack," said Fred, "Could you make sure I get home alright. I'm not feeling quite myself."

"You don't think I can get you home?" said Alice. "I got you here safely, didn't I?"

"Of course you did. That's very kind of you. If you think you can manage, I would love to have you take me home. When ever you are ready, I am."

"I think I should get Fred home; or someplace;" Alice stood up, "Come on Fred. You ready to go?"

Fred tot up, followed Alice out. She led him out to a city street, to her car.

The two got in. Alice drove slowly down the narrow street.

"What's this about a dream?"

"It's hard to describe. It is so strange."

"How are you feeling, anyway, Fred? You aren't ill, are you?"

"No, not as far as I know."

"That's the best any of us can do."

Alice drove in silence. She reached an apartment house. Fred got out. "You sure you're alright?"

"Yes, and thanks so much, Alice. That was a nice party."

"Yes, it was. I am glad you enjoyed it. I was worried. I'll see you tomorrow I suppose. Good night, Fred."

Alice drove off. Fred went into the building. He walked up a flight of stairs, turned. There was his door. He got a key from his pocket, unlocked the door and went in. Everything inside his apartment was familiar. It was coming back, that fragment of a memory. He was a refrigerator salesman. But where? He went to an address book.

There was no familiar address anywhere inside. But it was a company address book. There was the address he wanted on the outside cover. Of course.

Fred, the next morning, got up. His alarm woke him at six and he was wide awake; but still, it seemed, dreamed. It seemed he was someone else, not Fred at all; but who, he couldn't quite remember. Silly, of course he was Fred. He finished breakfast, left for work. On his left, as he walked down the street, was a newsstand. He walked in.

"Good morning. Would you direct me to this address?"

"Good morning, Mr. Abernathy. Go down to the third traffic light, turn right. How else would you get there? Are you pulling my leg, Mr. Abernathy? Of course, that's where you work. You're being funny, Mr. Abernathy."

"Anyway, thank you."

Mr. Abernathy went to work. Yes, here was Alice. She was the secretary. "You are nice and early, Fred," she said.

Work was a problem. The selling came back; but there was, at best, a vague memory of his past there. People's names, other than Alice, had to be relearned. The days passed and things which he should have known kept cropping up.

"Fred, think you should get yourself a complete physical," said the company president.

Fred agreed he should. Then, several days later, Alice expressed some concern about him.

"Fred, you seem nervous and preoccupied," said Alice, "And you haven't, outside of work, spoken two words to any of your friends here. You need to relax a little and forget your worries, whatever they are. Mildred's been asking about you. What say we go over and see her tonight?"

Fred agreed to this. Several hours later found Fred at the house where he was when his memory first began giving him trouble. He and Alice went in. Mildred, that was her name, he remembered now, was glad to see them. She and Alice did most of the talking. Mildred fixed coffee.

"I was glad of the chance to meet Clairey," said Fred, "Quite attractive, isn't she?"

"Yes she is," said Alice. "That's not what has been worrying you? She's single. Why not ask her out?"

"Someday I just might," said Fred.

The conversation turned to other things. 'We should go," said Alice.

"It was a joy to see you," said Mildred. "Oh, by the way, Fred: You left your hat here, last time you were here. I wish you would take it with you, when you go. It's in the hall wardrobe."

Fred went out in the hall. There was the ancient wardrobe. It was a sinister looking old thing. Fred started to say, "No, I don't want the hat anymore. Please throw it out." But that would be silly. Fred opened the wardrobe.

There was a darkness behind the wardrobe. The wardrobe was the dark passage into a room. Fred stepped into the wardrobe. There, over his head, on a peg, was his hat.

"There it is," said Fred, but he couldn't reach for it. The wardrobe was a coffin.

Everyone was standing around it wide eyed, looking. A lady put a cuff link on each cuff. The minister closed the lid.

As We See the Stars

Albeit we think of stars as small things; a mere dust of light flakes which might add a glitter to midsummer fairy ring; or, perhaps, grace a Yuletide tree; chances are, this is not the fact of the matter. It seems to me that the star's small size is hearsay. Who has ever seen a star? Although stars do, time and again, fall; mostly, they effervesce in this less than pure air of night before they reach our world; or, perhaps, bum out with some pure cold flame; so that those that reach the earth at all, found greatly less than their former size, will indeed be mere sparkle, or dust. But what was that former size? We see the trees yonder on the distant hills. And we know them to be ten to twenty times the height of a man, yet they look to be small in size, as you or I might hold one or two of them in our hand. And how much further must be the stars from us than the trees? Ten? Twenty? One hundred times:? Very likely at least one hundred, and, perhaps, even two hundred times the distance to the trees on that most distant hill. The stars then must be at least the size of large dinner plates. Likely, many will be found the size of mill wheels. Maybe they vary in size from one to the other; from dinner plates to even larger than mill wheels, say, once and a half a large mill wheel.. I suspect this is the case. And the moon; if it should in truth be cheese; which I suspect, it is not; must be quite a cheese indeed. It should make a large enough hole should it happen to fall close by to Norwich; much as would this castle were it to fall from the sky onto those hills; though I doubt if the moon would be as heavy as all of that. I should think it would be more as if a dinner plate, as big around as this castle to its very outer walls, were to fall.

THE PENALTY FOR WRONGDOING

"This is a wonderlul universe", said God. "I think; until at about the age of seven or eight, when they begin to learn how to underappreciate it; your son would have liked it; appreciated being born into it. I do not, as medievalists would have me do, toss persons into flaming hells where, for an eternity, devils stick red hot pitchforks into their butts. However, I think you will agree, there should be some penalty involved for wrongdoing. A walk appeals to me, to Andromeda. And, of course, back again."

By the time the young lady got to Andromeda, that galaxy had blown apart; so, no longer existed. On her return to her starting point; whole hatfulls of suns had been born and died. Her heart sank when she heard God say, ""I've been thinking, that was nothing but a short little stroll. We have time for a trillion strolls to where Andromeda was, have we not? Yes, take a trillion walks. If I were you, I'd keep count, so that you will know when you have completed walk number one trillion." As the program terminated; the trillionth walk came to an end.

"You will find it difficult to locate ghost Earth among the ghosts of deceased planets. More so, I should think, than sifting to find one grain of sand among all of Earth's oceans. I might suggest, you think of distinguishing features. Your clue might be some small thing like a poem by Edward Lear:

"O my aged Uncle Arley sitting on a heap of barley in the middle of the night, on his nose there was a cricket; in his hat, a railway ticket, but his shoes were still too tight."

THE LONG DARK SADNESS

She was young Her trim body would walk those fields Swim naked in those waters Be warm and laughing like the birds She didn't look good in death. Illness was not kind. And I was glad to know these elements were recycled to tough fibered weeds. To life desiring insects To sex filled animals But while she lived even at the last There was too much of sky There were too many birds in her eye To wish her gone. They buried Janet in the rusty earth Many times we had conversed together

And she wanted to live Live like the perpetual birds To fly over rivers and fields And in the season Find just the right shade of straw for the nest I say this Yet relate more to Discovering just the proper flavor of cheese For my apple pie In Deedle's Tavern with my Bohemian Beer The faded picture of Old Rockville on the wall Old Mr. Bo Winking from the Bohemian Beer advertisement over the bar. My beer would seem Pretty thin Spread as an electron strand across the stars And there With sparks of fire Myself running that endless dark trip Through mad patterns blindly whirling. As with all fundamental forces I coil and whip my little tears for life that fall Blending with the waters that drip through vast space The split electrons stuttering into some distant time One by one to feel the flash of brilliant knives That strip the cover off electric pain The vertebrae from some crystal chain Or may split again some virgin lip Janet is dead Now the silent black is above her. I see life still silhouettes the sky And I think not much over her earth And can't relate to her past thoughts And can't project her thoughts into the now happenings But am sad at the long silence The diffuseness one must suffer to be birds Now the bitter green. Not more bitter for Janet lying there Than for those of Ancient Greece Of Ancient Tyre Than for hairy Neanderthal who On some cold day Struggled with old rock And my thoughts struggle with the bitterness of worms With the bitterness of lungfish struggling desperately From some ancient sea With the bitterness of isolated stars With the chained mass of blind matter On the long dark trip to break Free into the joy of things that know the verb To be

Floating in a Dream

The ice would crack slightly.
It wouldn't move,
Not one second further
Through time.
The sky with its sort of clouds
Would color the ice
A wet gray.
One could be certain
The grass would be uncut.
One could see it there
Curled beneath the ice.
The ice would lie,
A long patch
Surrounded by speckled,
Tramped-on snow.
One would see it again in dream
As a fish
That swims in and out
And mirrors itself
On sleep.

Afterward

"A man of words instead of deeds is like a garden full of weeds", might be construed, a compliment.

Often; while becoming occupied in examining random sections of the matter about me; often too, while recording my discoveries of harmonies, stresses, contrasts and of the varieties in form and texture; things found in all matter; I find myself spend ing a lot of time examining and recording the condition of weeds. I notice my writing becoming weedy. I, myself, don't mind this condition. One of my former neighbors kept a neatly mowed back lawn. My other, allowed hers to grow up in weeds. My lawn, I split down the middle; thereby, keeping my peace with the lady who liked to look at mowed grass; at the same time, keeping a harmony with the other, with the unmowed lawn. For my aesthetic pleasures, and for my inspiration, I looked upon my weedy section of lawn. The weeds shaped themselves in a quantity of different forms and textures, a variety pleasing to behold. Then, while enjoying them aesthetically; I benefited, also from the bit of leisure; the time which I spent in their company. Then too, as such things as the end of the season fragrance of ragweeds and meadow asters drifts onto my pages, I get the longer visit with the characters which inhabit my writings. And I may keep a longer company with my readers. This lingering, in my writings, among my weeds, this bit of leisure; is to me, a relief from furious action. I don't strive to entertain my friends with a stream of continuous actions or jokes; but, to entertain with a relaxed companionship; an easy conversation; or maybe, just an evening smoking our pipes together. Furious, action packed writing is inclined to my way of thinking, to take life out of perspective. That sort of writing is inclined to abdicate from the ability of being able to tell the reader of something a little out of the ordinary happening and of having it seem a little out of the ordinary. Even in the most magical stories, I like to think of the people in them as, much like ourselves, usually concerned with everyday things. The inclusion, in these stories, of the tough fiber of everyday things; the descriptions of the weed filled pathways; of the dust covered stones of buildings; warped, weathered boards of gates, of fragrance and tastes of the dinners; lends a credibility to things strange, magical, uncanny; which might occur in the stories. I can't, of course, bring actual weeds, boards, and stones to my readers. Nor, even bring, to the reader, more than a hint of what is the form and texture of these things, a hint of the form and texture and of the things relationships to other things. Mostly, I rely upon the recall of the reader to fill in the details from similar past experiences of his own; to fill in, also his feeling s about these tings, feelings derived from past associations. By the use of his stones, boards, weeds; together with the use of mine; we can share experi ences among those things. Not the exact experiences, of course, for each experiences a most individual thing; but similar experiences. The difficulty comes when the writer, with his audience, has fewer and fewer experiences in common to share. We, with our experience among subdued and finite bits of forest, would have difficulty in relating to the writers of old when they wrote of their infinite forests, untamed as they were, and untamable. The recent path has eliminated the great stretches of unspoiled nature between towns. A field of flowers is only that until it comes to the next highway. The indescribably joy in the freedom of flowers, in their endless fields, is no more. No more the anticipation of further pleasure as one walks up each successive hill, but an anxiety lest the far side be spoiled by the encroachments of civilization. IF the future, wit hits weed killers and trim lawns, renders my weedy paths a thing of the past; if the few remaining weeds peek like caged animals from behind inaccessible stones, I will have lost a communication with the readers of that future. However, I am not my writings; my tales, my histories, my poetry. On that future date when my readers have no weeds of their own; I'll be somewhere else, somewhere with my vast conglomeration of unrecordable awarenesses, those ever changing awarenesses like those of shifting lights in sunny weed filled fields. I'll be alone in those otherwise uninhabited and uninhabit able fields, in some unapproachable place with the secret delights of my weeds.

Farewell to Linden Hill

The ladies' voices talk on, talk quietly as slumbering brooks over the pebbles run. Among late evening's darkening shadows, the babble flows. And the ladies rock as they talk. Touched with the fading light, purple and pink from the sunset, the ladies rock on. The wind rattles the loose boards of an old grey farm house on the brink of oblivion. But it will hang forever as part of the eternal past which can never be annihi lated. And the simes will forever look down. To find them, one need only to reel back time. In their place in space and time, one might find the old grey farm house and in the sky over it, over it looking down, the simes.

GOOD NIGHT

The Moon dips gently toward the West;

Not full, when in her regal gown she's dressed,

But now at half,

One sees she wears,

Instead, a gauze thin shift.

She's on her way

to bed.

— Finis —

191

www.ingramcontent.com/pod-product-compliance
Lightning Source LLC
Chambersburg PA
CBHW050846180626
46814CB00007B/2638